# Twisted Fairy Tales

A Quantum Book

Copyright © 2012 Quantum Publishing

First edition for North America and the Philippines published in 2013 by
Barron's Educational Series, Inc.

All inquiries should be addressed to:
Barron's Educational Series, Inc.
250 Wireless Boulevard
Hauppauge, New York 11788
WWW.BARRONSEDUC.COM

ISBN: 978-0-7641-6588-7

Library of Congress Control Number: 2012943308

This book is published and produced by
Quantum Books
6 Blundell Street
London N7 9BH

QUMTWFT

Publisher: Sarah Bloxham
Managing Editor: Samantha Warrington
Assistant Editor: Jo Morley
Editorial Assistant: Rebecca Cave
Production Manager: Rohana Yusof
Author: Maura McHugh
http://splinister.com/
Illustrator: Jane Laurie, www.janelaurie.com
Design: Martin Stiff, www.amazing15.com

Date of Manufacture: September 2012
Printed in Huizhou, China by 1010 Printing International Ltd
9 8 7 6 5 4 3 2 1

# Twisted Fairy Tales

### Maura McHugh

*Illustrated by*
### Jane Laurie

BARRON'S

# Contents

# Snow White

"Annabel, your skin is a fresh spring apple, pink and fragrant, urging my lips to kiss it," the King whispered as he undressed his beautiful new Queen on their wedding night. The awe and reverence in King Robert's tone calmed her nerves. Throughout their courtship, all her focus had been on securing his affections and becoming his wife, despite the keen competition from other ladies of the court. Now, the priest had sealed the union, the feasts were over, and she could finally relax and enjoy her reward.

"We will make the prettiest babies in the land," the King added, peeling a camisole spun from spider silk from her breasts. She tensed.

Annabel was pregnant again. She could not bear the terror in her heart every time the baby turned inside her. Would this one survive? Two other babies had been born — dark-haired boys — and they had both died: one stillborn, while the other only lasted a single heart-wrenching night.

Everyone spoke in hushed tones around her, and Robert had ordered her to remain in the castle, despite the stifling heat of summer. Annabel sat, miserable and sweating, in her private chamber, holding the scrying mirror her mother gave her when she thirteen. Her mother had groomed her for marriage from the moment Annabel's promise of beauty had unfurled into its full potential. There had been an endless array of tonics and skin lotions, as well as lessons in elocution, deportment, etiquette, duty and obligation. Every night, she had gone to bed thinking only how to project the best image of lovely, untainted womanhood, with just enough spirit to engage a suitor without appearing too ungovernable.

Lately, Annabel had seen the looks the other women

had been giving her husband. Until she produced a child, she wasn't safe. She kept up the rigorous beauty regimes, and the King remained entranced by her. But that would not last for ever.

She glanced down at the mirror in her hand. It was carved from ebony wood with a handle that mimicked the branch of a hawthorn tree, heavy with flowers. Only if you peered closely could you see the sly, knowing faces carved amid the blossoms. Annabel's mother had known many charms and spells, and had taught them all to her. "The women in our family could always seduce luck and bend fortunes," her mother had confided.

Suddenly determined, Annabel picked up the silver comb from her dressing table and stabbed it into the heel of her palm. A row of ruby blood beads emerged on her white skin.

She flung the offering onto the mirror's surface and lifted the mirror with her aching hand. She could feel the rustling of the flowers in the handle and the quiet murmur of voices from those that dwelled within. Then she uttered:

"Mirror, Mirror, tell no lies,
Will my child live and thrive?"

The blood on the glass slicked across to form a thin red surface. Tiny faces and mouths swam inside the pool. They spoke in a single chorus of shrill voices:

"Your child will be hale and healthy,
Your husband secure with love's fidelity."

Annabel released a long sigh. At last, she could rest easy. But the mirror stirred under her hand, as if it had heard her thoughts.

"Beware, lovely Queen, prettiest of them all,
Your reign will end when your beauty falls."

The baby kicked in her belly, causing Annabel to start.

She is the fairest girl I have ever seen!" gushed Robert, cradling the baby in his arms and swinging her gently. "She doesn't even cry. She's already a lady."

He stood by the window in their bedroom, allowing the pale winter sunlight to bath their daughter's features. Annabel lay exhausted in her bed. The birth had been hard. She'd heard the midwives' fearful prognosis at one point, and ordered them to fetch her mirror. For the rest of her labor, she gripped its handle and screamed her defiance when she felt the shadow of death place cold hands upon her. The mirror opened the path, allowing the baby out into the world and Annabel to remain in it.

The Queen watched the nurses and midwives gather around Robert and the child like fussing mother hens.

"A name..." she whispered, forcing the words from a throat, hoarse from yelling.

Robert stared out of the window at the landscape, mantled in the first snowfall of winter.

"Snow White," he declared, and the women clapped their approval. "Send forth a proclamation," he added. "Princess Snow White has been born."

The Queen bridled at his presumption, but she also remembered the blood on her bedding and on the surface of her mirror, so she said nothing.

A midwife bustled over to her and placed a cooling cloth on her forehead. "Rest, my Queen," she said. "You need to regain your strength. You look so fatigued."

For the first time, Annabel noticed the plump, fresh cheeks of this handsome woman, and her curls of chestnut hair.

She pulled herself up, gritting her teeth against the daggers of pain. "Fetch my handmaiden," she ordered. "I need to be presentable for my daughter."

The King smiled at his Queen and nodded in approval.

There were no more children. Snow White's birth had made that impossible. Robert didn't care, for he doted on his daughter and treated her as his heir in all ways - even teaching her skills that Annabel considered unsuitable for a girl. He spoiled her, Annabel realized, turning her against her mother.

*She liked to engage in mock battle with the beasts depicted in the tapestries.*

Snow White didn't want to sit by Annabel and hear stories of courtly love and allow her mother to brush her black hair. She fidgeted and rolled her eyes during the Queen's lessons on chivalry and fine manners. She complained at being forced to wear elaborate dresses or shoes that pinched her feet. She liked to dash down the hallways, her fine hair flying behind her, and engage in mock battle with the beasts depicted in the tapestries.

Worse still, her father often took part in these wild displays. They laughed in the same hearty, unaffected manner. They spoke with direct honesty that won people over, even when their words were sometimes too blunt or rash. Yet everyone agreed that Snow White had inherited her mother's beauty, and thankfully not her father's crooked nose.

After a while, Annabel stopped trying to engage her daughter in her interests. Instead she concentrated on being a good wife and a respectable queen. She embroidered with her handmaidens, pressed wild flowers, presided over the running of the royal household, and organized banquets for visiting dignitaries. Annabel's skills in staging elaborate balls became legendary, and everybody vied for a place on the guest list. She always had the most fashionable dress and outshone one and all. Women wished they were her, and men desired her. Annabel remained devoted to Robert, but in a distant way, aware that she had been supplanted in his affections.

Occasionally, Snow White would give Annabel a small morsel of her attention. Despite herself, the Queen craved those moments. For Snow White's sixteenth birthday, she organized a series of celebrations that took three months to prepare: sledges with wolf pelts to convey the guests to a skating party at the royal lake, fireworks to greet them at the castle, and later, an elaborate feast with entertainment followed by a ball in rooms decked out in gold and crystal.

Snow White allowed her mother to choose her dress. During the long fittings, for once Snow White didn't whine and proclaim herself bored. She asked questions about who would attend the party, and Annabel gladly regaled her with histories of the royal families who would gather in their home.

The Queen's heart warmed towards Snow White; perhaps her daughter was growing up and finally understood her future duties.

*The Queen woke the chef and declared that she had a sudden craving for lightly cooked viscera.*

Snow White's birthday was wondrous. When the Princess emerged at the ball, sumptuously coiffed and dressed, she stopped all conversation. Her gown was a miracle of white satin, lace, beads and embroidery. She was the first snowdrop, a herald of spring, despite winter's grip. Her unbound hair, glossy raven, streamed down her pale neck, and she was crowned with a diamond tiara. Annabel was brimming with pride at her achievement as her daughter took her father's hand and swept onto the ballroom floor for the opening dance of the night.

"She's breathtaking," the Queen overheard one courtier say as the music swelled and her husband and daughter danced past the admiring faces. But the smile on Annabel's face froze when she heard the snide response, "Perhaps Queen Annabel will begin to dress her age. She's no longer twenty-one." "She's not even thirty-one," sneered the other.

Annabel left the ballroom, and the light and laughter. She retired to her private room and took up the mirror in her bloodied palm.

"Mirror, mirror in my hand,
Who is the fairest in the land?"
The voices in the handle thrilled:
"While you are fair, it is true,
Snow White is now more beautiful than you."
Annabel remained in her room for the rest of the night, conversing with the mirror, and no one noticed that she was missing from the celebrations.

All spells require a sacrifice. "The greater the prize, the greater the price," Annabel's mother used to say. To achieve everlasting beauty and reign, the Queen required the heart and liver of her only daughter.

Annabel was conscious of her effect on men. She had been taught to manipulate them from an early age. Flattery, flirtation, cruelty, and bribery were all proven methods. "The easiest way to control men is through their vanity or their greed," Annabel's mother once told her. "Or through love, if you're lucky," she added.

So, Annabel took the trouble to learn about the huntsman before she met him. He was young, attractive, and had a new baby at home. He also liked to drink and gamble while drunk. His debtors were legion.

In the snowy woods, under a moonless sky, Annabel offered the huntsman enough money to solve all his problems in exchange for the life of Snow White. She charmed and cajoled and showed him the gold, until he forgot right from wrong and agreed to the task.

That very night, he stole Snow White from her bed and rode away with her through the woods until the trees became so thick that he was forced to dismount and find a safe path to a clearing in the heart of the forest.

Snow White didn't beg or plead. She wore no cloak or shoes, yet she didn't shiver. Starlight gleamed on her black hair, as if the stars hid among her tresses. She stood straight, her hands bound before her, and looked deep into the huntsman's eyes. In that moment, she possessed the icy, unearthly beauty of the forest spirits, whose stories he had grown up with. He shook his head, afraid that she was casting a spell upon him, and close by, a creature shrieked; in his mind, it was the cry of his lonely babe at home.

He shoved her away. "Go! And never return. Your mother wants you dead."

Her expression reminded him of a doe with an arrow in its heart. The huntsman turned and escaped her gaze.

When the huntsman deposited the bag with the liver and heart of a boar in front of the Queen, he declared with certainty that Snow White was dead — after all, no underdressed girl could survive the deepest woods locked in deadly winter.

The Queen woke the chef and declared that she had a sudden craving for lightly cooked viscera. As the sun rose, she cut slivers of the heart and liver, and imagined the beauty of her daughter suffusing her face and body. She smiled, her teeth tinted red.

When the alarm was raised about the King and Queen's missing daughter, Queen Annabel was radiant in her grief. King Robert threw himself into the search for Snow White. Armies and villages were mobilized, but the girl had vanished. The Queen spent much of her time in her private chamber, and several of her servants reported that they could hear her talking to thin air.

"She's mad with grief," they supposed, and in a way they were glad, for that seemed a reasonable response to the disappearance of a loved child.

The more the King was away, the more the Queen assumed his responsibilities. She understood the importance of budgeting and organization, yet, the councillors found her sometimes strange. She took to wearing a hand mirror, hung from a scarlet silken rope, around her waist. Sometimes she would stare into it while her councillors reported on the business of the land. When she turned her gaze upon them, afterwards they would recoil in dread. Always she would ask a perceptive question that would lead to a solution to the problem at hand.

The councillors did not like her rule, yet they could not identify why.

One of the kingdom's most pressing problems was a band of outlaws, living in the woods, who preyed upon the traffic on the King's road that skirted the tree line. They were clever and dangerous, and before long, songs and stories about them arose. The Queen ordered her army to wipe them out, but the outlaws knew the forest better than the soldiers.

Finally, they captured one of the robbers and he was hauled to the dungeons for questioning, despite being near death.

"We do it for her," he raved as they broke his fingers and stretched his limbs. "She is the fairest of them all."

The words troubled the Queen so she consulted her mirror. It replied:

"Widow Queen, you are fair, it is true,
But Snow White is more beautiful than you."

Her breath caught in her throat – "Widow Queen"? That afternoon, they brought home her husband's body. He had died in his tent the previous night, still intent on finding his lost daughter.

> "Widow Queen, you are fair, it is true, but Snow White is more beautiful than you."

The people whispered about a curse, and the vassal lords became unruly. Queen Annabel worked hard to remain in control of her kingdom, but with no husband and no heir, the neighboring lands believed her country to be weak and unprotected.

That night she discussed her plans with the mirror. It now needed more blood than she could afford, and so began the ugly job of offering others' blood. "Sacrifice is necessary," Annabel hummed to herself as she slit the throat of one of the kitchen maids — no one would miss her — everyone would assume she'd run off with some young suitor.

Annabel put on a cloak cast with a spell courtesy of the mirror. It made her appear as an old woman — the transformation was so uncanny that she touched her face in disgust. This is what awaited her if she didn't kill

Snow White.

She laced half an apple with poison and slipped out of the castle by a secret way known only to her. Then she traveled to the woods with her wicker basket of apples, hitching a ride from a miller who was transporting sacks of flour to the next town on his cart. She sat at the back, swinging her legs as the cart bumped over the recessions in the road. She felt strangely happy.

At the right place, Annabel jumped off the cart and found her way through the forest, as explained to her by the mirror. Hidden among a thick grove of trees, she discovered the ramshackle house, its chimney puffing smoke, and heard the sound of singing.

There was Snow White, sweeping out the house, with the smell of baking bread wafting gently. A row of men's shirts flapped on a clothes line. Everything the mirror had foretold was true: Snow White was alone.

Annabel squeezed her eyes as if shortsighted, hunched her back, and hobbled towards Snow White.

"Good afternoon, madam," Snow White called out, wiping dust from her cheek. "I don't see many travelers here."

"I'm visiting my sons who are felling wood, and I saw the smoke rising from your house." Annabel replied, stepping closer to Snow White so she could get a good look at her daughter — the change in circumstances had not impinged upon her beauty. "Care to buy some apples, dearie?" Annabel asked, her voice thready with age.

Snow White cocked her head and appraised the basket of apples. It was such a familiar movement to Annabel, one that Robert had done a hundred times. For an instant, her resolve wavered. Then the aches of the old, feeble body assaulted her, and she recalled her purpose.

Annabel picked up the glossiest, most inviting apple of the bunch. "Let us share one so you know they are worth buying." She drew a dagger and cut the apple deftly in half, then offered one slice to Snow White. The other she bit into immediately, savouring its sweet juices.

Snow White crunched into the apple and in that moment she recognized her mother. Her eyes widened in shock, but quickly a dull glaze crept over them as the effects of the poison seized her.

She fell to the ground with a thud.

There could be no mistake about it: she was dead.

Inside her heart, Annabel felt a dreadful tearing followed by a calm emptiness. She raised her dagger. Now for the butchery...

In the distance, deep voices rang out in song.

Cursing, Annabel retreated, knowing she could not gut her daughter and get away before the men arrived. She would have to find another way to maintain her beauty and halt her decline. At last, however, Snow White was dead, and Annabel would rule as Queen without a care.

## Snow White

Annabel took nothing for granted on this occasion, but the mirror confirmed that Snow White was gone from this world. As the years rolled past, the Queen heard rumors of a shrine in the forest, in which a dead girl, encased in a crystal casket, miraculously didn't wither. The glass coffin was in the heart of outlaw land, however, so few risked robbery to visit. It lent the story even more allure and mystery. Among young noblemen it became a daring adventure to seek out the dead maiden, and many of them returned penniless and humiliated as a result. Yet that did not deter them.

The Queen learned of different sacrifices to hold onto her good looks; all of them involved blood. Along with her beauty regimes, there was also the monthly sacrifice of a virgin boy or girl on the dark moon and her own constant bloodletting to fuel the hexes that kept her council in check and ensured friendly relations with neighboring countries.

At first, she found the murders difficult and dosed her victims with strong narcotics to ensure their submission. As time advanced, she realized that their struggles for life increased the magic. Eventually she waited eagerly for the dark moon, when she could slip on her black robes and listen to the young plead for mercy.

The castle gradually became a quiet and somber place. Annabel had little time for banquets any more, but the few she staged were macabre events, with unwholesome entertainment and unsavoury decorations. No one competed for those invitations. Around her settled a shroud of dread, and those who openly spoke about her fearful reputation had a tendency to succumb to a mystery illness and disease.

One day, in a batch of communications, an invitation arrived for Queen Annabel to attend the marriage of a Prince Rupert to a young Princess, named Snow White, in a distant land. Annabel rushed from the council chamber, and in her bedroom took up her mirror. It recounted the tale:

"Dark Queen, it was a mysterious hiccup.
The apple dislodged and Snow White woke up!"

In her fury Annabel smashed the mirror against the wall, and it splintered into thousands of fragments. Howls of triumph echoed in her room, and a whirlwind of invisible sprits rushed around her. Unseen fingers raked through her hair and yanked it.

"For releasing us from the mirror kingdom
You will no longer ever be without our wisdom."

They laughed and giggled, shrieked and wailed, slapped her face, and sang songs of death and torture to her all night long.

After the wedding of Prince Rupert and Princess Snow White, guests from kingdoms far and wide assembled for a festive banquet. Snow White wore an elegant, simple dress, with a crown of daisies and a forest of wild flowers in her hair, and the Prince sported his dashing scarlet and gold soldier's uniform. A company of rather rude and uncouth men occupied one table at the back, but the Princess would hear no criticism of their bawdy songs and large appetites. Instead she laughed and joked with them, and raised toasts in their honor. Several of the more refined guests sniffed their noses in disgust or raised their well-plucked eyebrows at this behavior. Behind their hands, a few of them mumbled that Prince Rupert might have future problems with his outspoken bride.

After the meal, the royal guests lined up to pay their respects to the happy couple and present their gifts. As their numbers dwindled, a carriage pulled up outside and a final guest alighted.

Queen Annabel remained a beauty beneath the marks on her face, a dishevelled wig and an ill-fitting dress, but she seemed distracted and her gaze darted about. Once or twice she hissed at something that no one else could discern, and slapped at the air as if waving off flies.

When she stepped in front of Snow White and her new husband, a long and frigid silence reigned. Snow White gripped her husband's hand with white knuckles, and he glared at his mother-in-law with a merciless expression.

"I have brought a gift," said Annabel.

The assembly, hushed by the tension, leaned forward.

Annabel grinned a strange, slanted smile. "Revenge," and she bowed her head as if offering her neck, but kept her maniacal stare upon the couple.

"Seize her!" the Prince bellowed, and the guards rushed to grab Annabel. "We will make her dance for us on our wedding day," Rupert declared.

Soon the blacksmith entered the hall, holding the red-hot iron shoes by long tongs. No one had suffered this punishment for centuries.

They were laid in front of Annabel. Two guards gripped her arms and lifted her in the air while a servant removed her footwear.

They slowly lowered her into the sizzling shoes.

Annabel screamed, and her agonized cries rolled around the wedding hall. She took one hobbling step and threw her arms above her head before shambling towards the Prince and Princess in the worst mockery of a celebration dance.

All the while the heat from the shoes traveled up her legs into her body, for they were enchanted with old magic. Wisps of dark smoke rose from Annabel's dress and lopsided wig. She shrieked and twirled before the

> The Queen learned of different sacrifices to hold onto her good looks; all of them involved blood.

royal gathering.

The guests covered their mouths against the stench of cooked flesh and averted their eyes. Not even Prince Rupert could watch as the blackened, smoldering woman danced towards them with clanging steps.

But Snow White and Annabel were locked in each other's gazes throughout the ordeal.

Finally, Annabel fell upon the steps in front of her daughter's throne. One crisped arm extended to touch Snow White's shoe, but she edged it backwards to avoid contact.

Annabel's last gasped words were suffused with ashes: "You are your mother's daughter."

In a quick and deadly movement, Snow White drew her husband's sword and pierced her mother's throat, stopping her cries and her pain.

"At least I have mercy," she said.

Snow White turned her face away at last, this time to hide a single tear, rolling down her graceful cheek.

# The Bone Whistle

Long ago, in a kingdom far away, a queen ruled her people. Years earlier her husband had died in a battle in a foreign realm, leaving her to run the country and bring up their twin son and daughter, Arthur and Ava. Despite her fears and the suspicions of her government, the Queen proved to be a wise and strategic leader.

Her children were educated well and given the finest clothes and best entertainment, although they didn't see their mother often because a queen must work very hard.

One day, not long after they turned thirteen, the twins fell to arguing about who would inherit their mother's position.

"Naturally, it will be me," claimed Arthur, and stuck his chin up in a smug fashion.

They were sitting at the large oak table in the small dining room, waiting for their mother to join them for supper.

"And why are you so sure of that?" asked Ava, glaring at her brother. "I was born before you."

"By only two minutes," he said hotly. Ava's earlier appearance was always a point of contention between them.

"I was first."

Arthur waved his hand, dismissing her argument. "It won't make any difference. I'm going to be king."

"What's this? Plans to replace me already?"

Their mother had walked into the room unnoticed while they were arguing. The children stood up politely, and waited until she took her place at the head of the table before sitting down again. They began their meal of roast boar and potatoes, eating in silence.

Eventually, Arthur spoke up. "Mother, tell Ava that I'm going to be king after you die."

"I haven't decided who will rule after me," the Queen replied gravely, and took a sip of her wine. "And I hope I won't have to make that decision for a long time."

Arthur speared a plum with his dagger. "After you die, the council will name me king." He spoke with absolute confidence.

The Queen regarded her son and realized that he voiced the truth. The decision would be made by others if she did not make a choice beforehand, since, as she had learned, death sometimes arrived unheralded. She watched the twins for the rest of the meal. Both had fine qualities. Arthur had his father's fair looks and her easy temperament, while Ava had inherited the Queen's dark features and her father's quiet observation. The Queen could not choose between them.

The following day, she summoned the children to her study. They stared around at the room full of maps and ledgers, for they were never allowed in that room. The Queen sat in a large chair with armrests carved in the likeness of dragons. Her eyes were shadowed, as if she had not slept well.

"You were right, Arthur," she said. "I must come to a decision about who will rule after I'm gone. There is a lot to learn about governing a country, and you are old enough to assume some duties."

Arthur and Ava stood up straight and glanced at each other from the corners of their eyes.

"I am setting you a task. There is a rare flower that blooms at this time of the year called Royal Beauty. The first of you to find the flower and bring it to me will rule when my reign ends."

The children bombarded their mother with questions, but she refused to tell them more. "Go now," was all she said, and they had not seen her look so sad, or so serious,

since the news of their father's death.

Arthur dashed from the room and headed for the castle's vast library. He knew there was a section on botany, and he was confident that one of the large illustrated manuscripts would show him what the flower looked like and where to find it. He shoved chairs against the library doors so his sister could not enter.

Ava returned to her bedroom, put on her sturdiest clothes and best cloak, then went down to the gardens. She had a faint memory of walking there with her father and him telling her that old Henry, the head gardener, was the most knowledgeable person in the land about plants. She found the gardener weeding the carrots and asked him about Royal Beauty.

He scratched his large red nose, and nodded. "Aye, I know that flower. It's small, with five scarlet petals and a spiky green stem." He told her that it flowered in the morning and described the soil in which it grew. He even revealed where he last saw it bloom.

Ava went to the kitchen, packed some food, and set out for the stables. She said nothing to anyone about her mission.

In the library, Arthur was not having much luck. He liked to hunt more than read books, and quickly became frustrated with dragging out large, dusty tomes, many of which were illegible or written in strange languages. He opened a window to get a breath of clean air and spied his

> "There is a rare flower that blooms at this time of the year called Royal Beauty."

sister on her horse, leaving the castle. Furious at losing any advantage, he ran down to the stables, but no one could tell him her destination. However, he was a keen rider and an adept tracker, so he quickly saddled up his horse and gave chase.

It took Arthur some time to find Ava's trail, but he got lucky when he questioned a traveling monk who had seen her take a small path away from the Queen's road. Once he closed the distance, he hung back so she would not know he was following her.

Ava set up camp in a small grove of trees on top of a long mound. Her distant fire winked at him, but he could not light one of his own for fear that she would see it. Arthur spent a cold, hungry night in the dark, listening to owls hooting and foxes yapping and hoping it would not rain.

As soon as the skies lightened at dawn, he crept closer to his sister's camp, using all the skills he had been taught. She ate bread and cheese, and he was afraid that the growling of his stomach would give him away. Ava tidied up and made for the side of the hill facing the sunrise. There, a sprinkling of small red flowers were unfurling to greet the sun. She picked them all and put them carefully into a pouch that hung from the belt around her waist.

Damp, starving, and frustrated, Arthur saw that he could not beat his sister. She was about to mount her horse when he stepped into the open.

"You didn't leave any flowers for me!" he said, angry.

"Would you have done otherwise?" Ava challenged.

He hated the fact that she knew him so well. He changed his tone to a persuasive one.

"Please, Ava, let us share them. We can ask Mother to name us co-rulers."

For a moment, Ava said nothing but looked hard at her brother. She shook her head. "No, you would not be satisfied to share. Once Mother is dead you might try to persuade the council to name you king. I've won the right to rule. Better to have it resolved now than disputed later."

Arthur grabbed the reins of her horse. It startled at his sudden movement and edged back.

"I'm not so devious!" he shouted.

"So, you didn't follow me instead of discovering how to find the flower on your own?"

He slapped her across the face. Fury and guilt warred inside him, but he also noticed the new coldness in her expression, the shift of her feet, and her hand twitch towards her dagger.

"Give me the pouch!" he demanded, and made a grab at it, hoping to act before she drew the weapon.

The horse neighed loudly and backed away from the children. Quick as a whippet, Ava had her dagger out and waved it at him.

"Stay away!" she warned, and moved backwards towards her horse.

Ava stumbled on a tuft of grass and Arthur saw his

chance. He dove at her, knocking her to the ground. She let out a high, piercing scream. He jumped up, aghast, to see the dagger embedded to its hilt in her chest. Ava lay, trembling. Bubbles of blood popped as she opened her mouth.

"Arthur," she gasped, "help!" She sounded like she was drowning.

But Arthur did nothing. Instead, he waited and watched her shuddering subside and her skin take on the pale sheen of marble. Eventually, she was as still as a statue in the grass. Her wide-open eyes reflected the sky above. Arthur took the pouch of flowers from his sister's corpse, and buried her.

*H*e returned home with his prize, and his mother proclaimed him the winner. They awaited Ava's return, but despite many searches, she was never discovered. The Queen never forgave herself for putting her daughter in harm's way. Arthur became melancholic and brooding, and everyone said the disappearance of his sister changed him into a cold and heartless person.

Many years later, a shepherd boy, in search of a wandering sheep, walked over Ava's unmarked grave and saw a bone sticking out of the earth. He picked it up and that night carved holes into the bone, with the idle thought of playing a few notes during the lonely days and nights he guarded his sheep.

When the shepherd blew into the bone whistle, it sounded like the sorrowful singing of a young girl. Surprised, he kept playing and the voice of Ava sang the song of her brother's betrayal. The pain in her voice brought tears to the boy's eyes.

He never told anyone about the voice in the instrument he had fashioned until one day, as he was playing the pipe, a knight from the Queen's court passed by. The knight recognized the voice and rushed to the boy, expecting to find the missing princess. It wasn't until the knight played the bone whistle himself, and heard it sing with Ava's voice, that he believed the shepherd's story.

The knight promptly returned to the castle and begged an audience with the Queen. Before the Queen and Arthur, he blew into the whistle, and Ava's voice sang of her death at the hands of her brother.

When the shocked queen turned to question her son, the fear and shame etched on his face explained it all. She could not bear to kill him. Instead, Arthur was walled up in a suite of rooms in the castle. Meals were passed in through a small opening three times daily. The Queen commanded that the shepherd sit by Arthur's suite each evening and play the bone whistle.

There are those who say the whistle did not sing for the prince. Instead it only screamed, high and piercing.

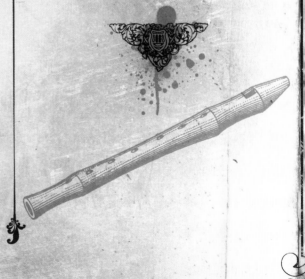

# Rapunzel

Rose and Karl lived next door to the village witch, Mother Melanie, and this was both a blessing and a curse. After the young couple had spent years trying to have a child, they turned to Mother Melanie for help. She provided Rose with the potions and advice that allowed her to conceive, and the couple were delighted and grateful. However, the old dame had a quick temper and was easily offended. If any of the villagers annoyed her, the unfortunate person soon developed an affliction, which was only remedied by an expensive cure in her cottage, set in its walled garden. "Mother Melanie always gets her price," they said.

The more Rose's belly grew round with the couple's much-anticipated child, the more she craved delicacies. Karl strove to satisfy her needs. One day, Rose desired a rare plant called Rapunzel, but no one in the village could provide it. Rose complained mightily. The next morning, Karl was shifting stones onto a small hillock at the back of their house when he spied Rapunzel growing in Mother Melanie's garden.

That night he slipped over the wall and snipped a couple of plants, taking care to ensure they would not be missed. Rose's delight at eating the plant overcame his fear after stealing from Mother Melanie. But the following day, Rose desired Rapunzel even more, and Karl could not bare her misery. Once again he crept into the witch's garden and helped himself to the plant. Rose glowed with contentment, and Karl's worries faded.

Another night came and the moon was fat and bright, and again Rose insisted on a bowl of Rapunzel. "One final time," she begged, and Karl couldn't deny her wish. He scaled the wall and crept to the patch of Rapunzel. He was kneeling in the damp soil, his knife in his hand, when a shadow fell across his face.

Mother Melanie stood before him, her hawthorn cane in her hand, her dark eyes blazing.

"Your child will never know a father, for you will die for stealing from me," she proclaimed.

Frozen by fear, Karl watched her raise her cursing stick.

# Rapunzel

"Anything! I'll give you anything!" he cried. "Please spare me."

Mother Melanie paused, and a cunning look twisted her features. "Your child or your life."

At first Karl was too horrified to reply, but somehow, over the course of their conversation, he agreed to her terms. The old woman would preside over Rose's labor and tell her the child had died.

"Don't worry, you'll have another," she promised. "As long as you never cross me again." Her dreadful gaze fixed him to the spot. "If you do, then all your family will perish."

So it came to pass that Rose had a long, difficult labor, which resulted in a stillborn girl. The entire village commented on how lucky Rose was to have had Mother Melanie in attendance, for she surely would have died otherwise. After a period of mourning, Rose conceived again and gave birth to healthy twins.

In fact, the witch had whisked the babe away to her cabin in the woods, where she cast her strongest magic spell. She named the girl Rapunzel, and intended to teach the child the arts that Mother Melanie had been taught by her own mother. From an early age, Rapunzel could sing to birds and understand their conversation. She had an uncanny talent for recognizing plants, and became adept at brewing potions and mixing ointments according to the old woman's instructions.

The villagers commented that as she aged, Mother Melanie's talents were getting stronger, for her salves and charms were more effective. Every time a customer praised her for one of Rapunzel's potions, her heart grew cold towards the girl.

By the time Rapunzel turned thirteen, she was becoming a beautiful young woman. She was quiet and respectful, for she believed that Melanie was her mother. Rapunzel kept the cabin clean and tidy, cooked, and created all the concoctions. Her friends were the birds, and they always sang together.

Upon returning to the cabin late one afternoon, Mother Melanie discovered Rapunzel talking to a woodsman, who had heard her song and became infatuated by her beauty. For the first time, the witch recognized that she had a problem: Rapunzel was invaluable to her business, but she would eventually leave, of her own accord or with a man. She immediately seized upon a solution.

Mother Melanie invited the woodsman into their home for a cup of tea, which she asked Rapunzel to prepare. The girl was so distracted by the novelty of company that she didn't spot the witch slip an elixir into the man's drink. After a few mouthfuls, he turned pale and collapsed. Rapunzel tried to revive him, but he appeared to be dead.

"You've killed him!" Mother Melanie exclaimed. She revealed that she was not Rapunzel's true mother and claimed that Rapunzel was the child of an evil witch and that she had rescued her from a mob that killed her mother. "Now your true nature has manifested itself," she added spitefully.

Rapunzel collapsed, weeping. "You must destroy me for what I've done."

"No," Mother Melanie replied. "I will hide you where you cannot harm anyone."

The witch collected Rapunzel's few belongings and dragged her into the deepest, darkest part of the woods, where fierce creatures held dominion. There lay a high stone tower, with no door and only a small window on the third floor. The old woman put an ointment on her forehead, muttered a charm, and grabbed hold of the frightened girl. They rose through the air and stepped into the tower.

"You'll be safe here," said Mother Melanie, then left Rapunzel alone.

For years, Rapunzel lived in the tower on her own. After the first visit, the witch combed special oil into Rapunzel's flaxen hair. It caused it to grow at an unnatural rate, and Mother Melanie braided it into a strong rope. After a couple of months, it was thirty feet long. Whenever the old woman visited, she stood underneath the window and called out, "Rapunzel, Rapunzel, cast down your fair braid," then clambered up with the agility of an acrobat. When Rapunzel queried

why Mother Melanie no longer used the levitation spell, she responded cryptically, "Never enchant a broom to fly when you can walk."

Over time, Rapunzel came to know the tower's every chipped stone and creaky board like the back of her hand. In the winter she wrapped her long locks around her shivering body to keep warm. During summer, her tresses became a scratchy burden. Rapunzel had repeated nightmares in which her hair continued to grow until it filled up the tower and suffocated her.

Every full moon, Mother Melanie arrived with food and herbs, and told Rapunzel what potions to make. Every dark moon, the witch collected the full pots and jars. During these visits, she always mentioned how much it cost her to feed Rapunzel, and the risk she took by sheltering her.

On one occasion, overcome with anger, despair, and loneliness, Rapunzel cut off her hair. The witch squandered her magic to enter the tower by levitation, and reapplied the special oil. She quietly reminded Rapunzel of her crime and left for two months.

Rapunzel had to stretch her meager supplies, never knowing when — or if — Mother Melanie would return. Meanwhile, her hair grew back swiftly. She sang to the blackbirds and they fetched her berries, while the owls brought her mice and voles. It was barely enough. When the witch returned, Rapunzel had become delirious from starvation and lack of company. If it hadn't been for the water well on the ground floor, she would have perished.

Days passed. The birds told her stories of the outside world, and often assured her that she was kind and gentle. Rapunzel never believed them. She knew that she was born wicked and was better off isolated from the world, even if her heart yearned to join it.

One sunny morning, Rapunzel sat by the window singing. A young nobleman, named Lucien, was passing by on horseback and became enchanted. He sat on his impatient horse for hours watching Rapunzel sing so finely that all the birds replied to her melodies. He also witnessed the arrival of Mother Melanie and heard her call out, "Rapunzel, Rapunzel, cast down your fair braid." Lucien recognized the witch, for her fame as a healer had spread far, and she had grown wealthy from her business. He also knew the rumors about her more malign practices.

After Mother Melanie had departed, Lucien approached the base of the tower. He pitched his voice high like the old woman. "Rapunzel, Rapunzel, cast down your fair braid," he warbled.

When he appeared at the window, Rapunzel froze. Lucien raised his palms and told her he wished her no harm. He spoke to her softly for some time before she would reply, and then she warned him to leave. "I'm dangerous," was all she would say.

Every morning, Lucien visited Rapunzel and she grew to trust him. Eventually, in between tears, she revealed the story of how she had murdered a man. Lucien listened and told her what he knew of Mother Melanie, but Rapunzel thought he was mistaken. She refused to leave the tower. "I'm safer here," she urged.

Over the weeks, Mother Melanie noticed a change in Rapunzel. She seemed happier, and less intimidated by her. The witch decided to wait, hidden, and watch the tower. She spotted Lucien arriving and saw the couple embracing at the window.

In a cold fury, she lingered there until he left. Then she stood at the bottom of the tower and imitated his voice.

"My love," Rapunzel cried as the witch began to climb, "why have you returned so soon?"

When Mother Melanie stepped into the room, she slapped Rapunzel across the face and cut off her hair with one swipe of her dagger. Then she placed a forgetfulness spell on the girl and cast her into the forest. Rapunzel wandered the fearful woods in a daze, not knowing her name, and with no memory of Lucien.

The next dawn, Lucien signaled Rapunzel, and Mother Melanie threw down the severed braid for the young man to climb. When he stepped on the window sill, she placed her knife against his throat. "Rapunzel is dead," she snapped. "You will never see her face again." With that, she smeared ointment on his eyes and he was instantly blind.

> She knew that she was born wicked and was better off isolated from the world.

In his fear and anguish, Lucien grappled with the witch. His attack unbalanced her, and her feet became tangled up in the braid. They both fell backwards out of the window, but Lucien held onto the braid. He plummeted through the air, expecting – welcoming – death. There was a terrible crack, and the braid yanked. It pulled from his grasp, but he didn't fall far.

Lucien lay in the damp grass, in the shadows, expecting the witch to finish him off. Yet she never appeared.

The nobleman struggled to his feet and whistled for his horse. He mounted, clung to its neck, and urged it home. The pain of his broken heart hurt more than the loss of his sight.

Yet through the darkness he heard Rapunzel singing. At first, Lucien thought it was merely his mind projecting his dearest wish. He cried out, "Rapunzel! Rapunzel!" but she did not reply. Then his horse halted and her kind voice asked, "Are you all right, my lord?"

He wept tears of happiness and reached for her hand. In that moment, when the salt of his tears touched her skin, the witch's spell was banished. Rapunzel remembered her name, and her love. They fell into each other's arms.

When Rapunzel discovered that Lucien had been blinded, she kissed his eyes and told him she would make them better, for she was more skilled in healing than Mother Melanie had ever been. She found the right herbs and put together a salve that restored his sight.

Rapunzel insisted that they return to the tower, and they arrived at dusk. Hanging from the window, with Rapunzel's braid wrapped around her neck, Mother Melanie swung in the breeze. Her face was purple, her swollen tongue protruded, and the crows had already feasted on her eyes.

For a long time, the couple sat on the horse in silence. Rapunzel's arms wrapped tight around Lucien's waist. His heartbeat was a new song that she wanted to know forever.

Eventually, the evening star appeared in the indigo sky. "It's time to leave," she said.

# The Red Shoes

For as long as Karen could remember, there was only her and her mother, Rachel. "Two peas in a pod," Rachel would say, for they lived together in one room, and slept in the same bed. Rachel worked at the Lion and Lamb Pub as a cook, and when Karen was small she often played in the kitchen. It meant that at least Karen ate every day, for her mother usually drank her wages away. Karen often had to roll Rachel into bed late at night.

During the summer Karen went barefooted, and in the winter they could only afford ugly, wooden clogs, stuffed with cloth to keep their toes from freezing. The older Karen got the more her mother drank, and some evenings she even had to help Rachel home.

The shoemaker's wife, Sarah, was a kindhearted woman and was one of the few who didn't call Rachel names. One morning she saw Karen helping her mother home. It was obvious Rachel had been out all night – she was soaked, pale, and coughing badly. In her bare feet, Karen slipped in the mud several times as she led her mother home. Sarah decided to fashion Karen a pair of shoes from discarded scraps in her husband's workshop. She wasn't trained, but she had helped her husband enough to know the basics. The only material available was a bright red, so although the shoes were crude, they were colorful.

Karen treasured the shoes. She wore them every day, and cleaned them every night. But she had other worries. Her mother lost her job because she was too ill to work, and Karen had to remain indoors all day to nurse her. She hated the sick room smell and her mother's delirious cries. One night, after listening to her mother's moans for hours, Karen prayed she would pass away.

The next morning Karen tried to shake her mother awake, but Rachel was cold to the touch and silent. Karen cried over her mother's body for hours.

Since she had no money, the priest performed a short ceremony. The only people at the funeral were Karen and Sarah. Karen wore her threadbare red shoes for she had nothing else suitable. People pointed and whispered as she followed her mother's straw coffin on the back of the gravedigger's cart.

On that day a wealthy woman called Mrs. Larsson was passing by in her carriage. Mrs. Larsson's husband had died years earlier, and both their sons had been killed in wars. She noticed the scrawny girl following the pauper's coffin and heard the cruel talk about her and her mother. She decided to rescue the girl from a life of sin.

Mrs. Larsson approached the priest about adopting Karen, and everyone praised Mrs. Larsson for her munificence. No one asked Karen what she wanted. She was pleased to have a good home, but Mrs. Larsson was old-fashioned and religious. She never let Karen forget that she had "saved her from the gutter" – a phrase she used repeatedly.

The first thing she ordered Karen to do was burn her old red shoes, because "red was the devil's stain". Mrs Larsson was color-blind, but she had heard the gossip in the town, and she wanted it clear to everyone that she was putting Karen on the straight and narrow.

Karen cried as she tossed the shoes into the flames in front of Mrs. Larsson.

Karen settled into her new life quickly. She went to a convent school and enjoyed learning, but she was tormented every day by a couple of girls who made fun of her accent and her mother. At home with Mrs Larsson she was expected to be obedient and quiet, to study after school, and read the bible with Mrs. Larsson in the evenings. Other than school or church, the only other time Karen was allowed out was to accompany Mrs. Larsson on her shopping trips. At least once during each excursion, Mrs. Larsson would loudly proclaim to a stranger how she had rescued the child of a fallen woman. Karen came to dread those trips to town.

One time they were leaving the butcher's when a large, ornate carriage bearing the insignia of the king pulled up. Two soldiers escorted the queen and her daughter into a shop. Karen saw the princess clearly. She was close to Karen's age and wore a beautiful white coat embroidered with gold and scarlet thread, and she wore a pair of red, Moroccan-leather shoes. Karen looked down at her practical, black shoes and wished she had some spot of color in her life.

On the way home, Mrs. Larsson offered effusive praise for the Queen and the Princess. "The princess wore a pair of pretty red shoes," Karen said, expecting Mrs. Larsson to be scandalized.

Instead she said, "I'm sure they were imported from Paris. The queen is renowned for her good taste."

When Karen questioned Mrs. Larsson about why red shoes were respectable for a princess, the widow told Karen that different standards applied to royalty. "When you're a queen you can wear red shoes," Mrs. Larsson laughed.

As the years went by, Mrs. Larsson became frailer and Karen gained a little freedom. When it came time for Karen's confirmation, Mrs. Larsson was too unwell to accompany her on her shopping expedition, but she insisted that Karen purchase the best outfit, no matter the cost.

Karen enjoyed the power to examine, and buy, whatever she liked. After a lot of thought she bought a white lace dress, gloves, and stockings. When she consulted the shoemaker, the first shoes she noticed was a pair of red leather and satin slippers. The shoemaker told her that they had been designed for a famous dancer, but the shoes had been too small.

"I took those measurements myself, so I don't know why they didn't fit. And she had bought special material from Damascus. She was furious. I had to make her two other pairs for free."

Karen tried on the shoes, and they fit perfectly. She stood up in them, and felt lighter. She had an intense urge to dance, so she twirled a little.

The shoemaker scratched his head, but smiled at how well his creation worked. "You were made for each other," he said, cheerful to have sold them at last.

Karen hid the shoes at the back of her wardrobe, and decided she would wear her plain shoes to the confirmation. Whenever she was in the room on her own she would sneak the red shoes out and put them on. Then she would dance around her room, imagining being at a party and the center of attention. Mrs. Larsson was against dancing and parties on principle.

On the day of her confirmation Karen put on her new dress and her old black shoes. She peeked at the bright red slippers, desperate to wear them, but reluctantly put the box away.

When she walked down the stairs she heard a gasp of surprise from one of the maids. Karen checked to see if she had any stains on her clothing and noticed she was wearing the red slippers. She had no memory of putting them on.

But it was too late to change, for Mrs. Larsson was already at the front door, and she was a stickler about punctuality.

Karen walked out of the house wearing the red shoes. She was thrilled. They deserved to be shown in public.

She felt as though she was floating through the day on her beautiful shoes. Everyone in the church noticed her. When the organ rang out and the children's sweet voices were lifted in song, all Karen wanted to do was dance. She had to concentrate to prevent her feet from tapping when she

knelt at the altar to receive the blessing from the archbishop.

The hardest part of the day was to return home and take off the red shoes without giving them the opportunity to dance.

By breakfast Mrs. Larsson had heard the news from several neighbors, and because the widow had been present at the mass everyone assumed she had condoned Karen's choice of shoes. She was livid and spent half an hour detailing to Karen how badly she had insulted the woman who had saved her from the streets. Mrs. Larsson finished her tirade by saying, "You've got bad blood Karen, and none of it is mine, thank God!"

She ordered Karen to burn the shoes.

Part of Karen was unrepentant. In fact, a little voice inside her laughed when she saw the old woman's watery eyes blaze and her arthritic hands clench. She agreed to destroy the slippers but she knew it was a lie. She had never owned anything so beautiful before. To burn them would be to burn her own feet. Karen swore to herself she would keep them forever.

That evening Mrs. Larsson had a stroke, and lost the use of her legs. The doctor told Karen that he did not expect the widow to improve but she could live for many years. From that point on Karen was either at school or running up and down the stairs to cater to Mrs. Larsson. Confined to bed and with slurred speech, Mrs. Larsson lost all kindness and directed her ire at her adopted daughter. She blamed Karen for causing her illness, and threatened regularly to cut her

> She felt as though she was floating through the day on her beautiful shoes.

out of her will.

Karen was allowed out on her own twice a week: to order supplies for the house, and to attend church. Mrs. Larsson told Karen that she would do all in her power to ensure that Karen escaped damnation. She quizzed Karen afterwards on who attended mass and what news she had heard about the neighbors.

Karen became bolder at wearing her red shoes in public. She didn't dare wear them to school for the nuns would send her home immediately, but she often put them on when shopping in town, and even to go to church. Mrs. Larsson only received a few visitors, so Karen knew reports of her behavior did not reach the widow's ears.

One day as she was leaving the grocer's she spotted a strange man leaning against the doorway to the Lion and Lamb pub door. He had a curled mustache and a long, pointed beard, as well as a dashing outfit. He gazed at her intensely as she walked toward him. She noticed him turn his head to say something to the fellow beside him. Karen imagined him asking about her, and everyone in the pub knew her family history.

She marched past him, looking straight ahead determinedly. As she did he called out, "Those are lovely dancing shoes. It would be a shame not to use them." Karen glanced at him, and his eyes twinkled and he grinned at her. She blushed and looked away. She had been warned not to speak to men on the street.

Yet, she couldn't forget his words. That night, when the house was quiet, she put on the red shoes and danced around the room. Later, breathless, she flopped back on her bed and fell asleep with them on.

The next day was Sunday, so Karen didn't bother taking off her shoes and wore them to church. She saw the sidelong stares from many of the congregation, but ignored them.

The priest gave a sermon about the evils of vanity in women. Karen noticed many men who seemed exceedingly fond of their best Sunday clothing, yet there were no cautionary words for them.

After church no one wanted to speak to her. Even the priest pretended to be busy when she waited to thank him for the mass. As she hung about outside, alone in the crowd of people leaving the church, the man she had noticed in the street sidled up to her.

"You will find no merry tune here for your red shoes," he whispered to her. "A shame, for I would love to see you dance." His smile was irresistible.

Karen laughed a little, and danced a couple of steps for him. She dipped a small curtsy, and he clapped his hands. "You're shameless," he said, and she thought there was an admiring tone in his voice. So she danced another few steps, and this time she could not stop.

Her feet, encased in the red shoes, twirled, tapped, and jumped. Soon, a space grew around her and everyone turned to stare. The priest's face flushed with anger, and Karen knew he thought she was defying him in response to his sermon. A lone voice called out "Bravo," and she thought she saw the stranger smile among the group of frowning faces.

Desperately, she tried to stop, but her feet refused. She directed them towards the carriage that awaited her, but she could not get in because of the disobedient shoes. The driver had to pick her up and place her inside, and all the time Karen cried and told him she could not control her feet. Finally she was able to remove the shoes, and set them on the seat opposite her.

Upon her return home she stashed the red shoes at the back of her wardrobe, and for a long period she didn't wear them—except in dreams, where she received an invitation to a ball, put on her red shoes, and danced with a handsome man all night long. Sometimes he wore a suit of scarlet and gold. When they spun around the dance floor he put his mouth by her ear, and his breath was hot upon her neck, "Red is the color of life. It pounds in all of us," he whispered.

She would wake from that dream, and ache to put on the red shoes, but she was too afraid of what might happen.

Mrs. Larsson got progressively weaker, and Karen tried to smother her resentment and take care of the woman. For a time she was the kind of daughter Mrs. Larsson wanted: malleable, penitent, and grateful. Yet, the widow only heaped cruelty upon Karen. One evening, while Karen fed her soup, the widow glared at her and said, "You too will wither and die eventually!"

The next morning Mrs. Larsson slipped into a coma. The doctor told Karen that the old lady's death would occur in a matter of days. Karen went to her bedroom and cried for the loss of both of her mothers, despite their failings.

That afternoon, an invitation was delivered for a ball to celebrate the sixteenth birthday of one of Karen's school friends.

Karen stood at the bedside of Mrs. Larsson, and said, "Mrs. Larsson, I have been invited to Imelda's birthday dance. If you do not wish me to go, give me a sign."

The house was silent save for the ticking of the grandfather clock in the hallway.

Karen put on her best dress, and stared at the red shoes. It was the first occasion where it would be appropriate to wear them. *And finally, I can dance at a party!* she thought.

She slipped on the red shoes and admired them in the mirror before she ran down the stairs to the carriage outside.

The party was exactly as she imagined it: the room was decorated with white and crystal, and skilled musicians played all the popular songs. There were exquisite dishes and fabulous dresses. Imelda was radiant as a star as her father

led her out on the dance floor. Despite her excitement at being there, wearing her red shoes, a dull hollowness lodged in Karen's chest. Few people spoke to her, and everyone seemed to have family and friends around them.

She took the offered champagne, and danced with several men in the hopes she could flee the emptiness in her heart. At last the man she had met before swung her onto the dance floor. "You and those shoes are made for dancing," he said.

"I am wicked," she confessed to him, her words slurred, "everyone tells me so."

"I adore wicked women," he replied and pulled her closer. They danced together for the rest of the night.

After the musicians played their last notes, and the gathering clapped in appreciation, Karen's dance partner tried to convince her to accompany him home in his carriage. She danced away from him, and shook her head, which felt as light as a snowflake. Her feet seemed to float over the ground. "Play on," she called out to the musicians. She swayed, her arms outspread. The musicians continued to pack away their instruments, and the remaining guests tittered at Karen. "I want to dance forever," she sighed.

The man marched across the floor and seized her arm. "Enough," he said. "I will play you a lively tune in my chambers, but be quiet now and come along."

She shook off his grip with surprising strength. "You don't get to tell me what to do!" she yelled, suddenly furious.

The room fell silent. Karen's feet continued to dance. Under the weight of the onlookers' disapproval her head felt full of clanking chains. She tried to stop dancing, but her feet continued moving. The man made a grab for her again, but she leaped away.

"I can't stop!" she cried. "My feet, they won't obey."

Servants attempted to catch her, but she evaded them on

her nimble feet. The shoes danced her out of the mansion and into the moonless night. They danced her through briars, bushes, streams. All the time she called out for help until her voice became hoarse.

By morning she was mud-splattered, scratched, and exhausted but her feet danced on. At one point Karen grabbed onto a fence post, but it only kept her in one place while her feet struggled for release. She tried to hold to the post with one hand and remove her shoes with the other but she made a terrible discovery.

The red shoes had fused seamlessly to her feet. There was no way to separate them. In her shock she let go of the post and her feet took off down the road, spinning and jigging her into the town.

As she danced past Mrs. Larsson's house the undertakers delivered a coffin, and the maid wept on the doorstep. She wasn't allowed to stop. The shoes danced her past all her neighbors and school friends. Karen held out her arms, begging for aid, but they withdrew from her, and summoned the police.

But Karen had danced out of town in minutes, and her feet dragged her relentlessly through bogs, forests, and villages. She became known as "the mad dancer", and children chased after her and threw stones. Occasionally, she was able to pluck fruit and nuts from trees and shrubs, or grab a pie from a food stall as she rushed past.

She could not rest or sleep, and she had little choice over her route. Her feet, directed by the scarlet slippers, went where they wished.

Starving, delirious, and filthy, Karen was dragged to the church on the day of Mrs. Larsson's funeral. A little hope sparked in her. Perhaps she if she was able to go into the church and say a prayer the red shoes would be appeased, and release her.

When she danced up the church path a blazing figure in white appeared. It was Mrs. Larsson, but transfigured. Her eyes were flames and in her hand she brandished a sword to bar Karen's way. "Ungrateful child," she bellowed, "those shoes have taken possession of you. They will dance you to death."

"Please, tell them to let me go!" she cried, but the figure crashed its sword into the path showering sparks at her. Karen raised her arms in front of her face.

"No one else can loosen their grip on you," she roared, and the shoes took off, pulling Karen back to the wilderness.

Weeks passed. Karen became a tattered human rag dancing through lanes and meadows. Without sleep and little food or drink she barely recognized what was real and what were the projections of her fevered, fatigued brain.

Sometimes she danced through fields of fire, while demons capered around her, and other times angels sang hymns to soothe her. But every time she staggered near a church the threatening figure appeared, wielding its unforgiving sword.

Eventually she danced past a small cottage, and outside

a man chopped wood with a great axe. "Please," she begged, "cut off my feet for the shoes will give me no respite."

The man recognized her as the mad dancer, and pity filled his heart. Yet, he could not bring himself to maim the woman. Karen danced away, weeping. Twice more over the following days she lumbered past his home, and each time she cried for him to end her torment.

The third time he was ready. He grabbed her by the waist, and her legs thrashed against him, desperate to dance. He laid her feet upon his chopping block and with two quick, precise whacks cut her feet off at the ankle.

Karen screamed in agony, and her feet sprang up from the ground to dance while blood spurted from the stumps of their ankles. They pranced away as she blacked out.

Over the coming months, the woodsman, named Hugh, cared for her as she dangled between life and death. During this time, visions of Mrs. Larsson haunted her dreams. "You've bad blood," she shouted, and she swung the sword to cut off Karen's feet.

Hugh carved two feet out of wood for Karen, which she was able to attach to her legs with buckles and straps. With the aid of two canes she learned to move about again.

A year later she moved to a town and gained work in a kitchen. She sent Hugh money regularly as thanks for the great kindness he showed her.

On the first Sunday in her new town she attempted to attend church. As she clattered up to the driveway on her canes, her severed feet, clad in the red shoes, jumped out of the undergrowth and danced gleefully in front of her.

Karen cried out and staggered back. The other churchgoers shied away from the strange woman, and looked about for what scared her. Karen could not move past the red shoes and their mocking steps.

For years thereafter, every time Karen dared to approach a church, the red shoes would frolic before her, and prevent her passage.

During that time she devoted herself to her job, and taking care of the poorest in the town. Having been destitute and cast out, Karen understood the impact of a kind act on the desperate. She expected nothing in return, and spoke of it to no one, but over time her reputation as a caring person grew.

Yet, she could never forget the red shoes.

Many years later, as she lay upon her deathbed, she realized she wasn't alone. The people to whom she had shown compassion and friendship over the years ensured Karen was comfortable and cared for. Her last sight, before she exhaled her final breath, was the faces of dear friends.

As Karen slipped away, a luminous figure appeared before her. It was her mother Rachel. She touched Karen's cheek, and at once Karen was suffused with love and warmth.

Karen stood up, and miraculously her feet and legs were whole again.

"Forgiveness lies within," Rachel said.

Karen laughed. Now, it seemed so obvious.

"You were always Queen of my heart," her mother added. She held the first pair of red shoes in her hands. Scuffed, crooked, but crafted with love and care.

Karen put them on, and took her mother's hand. She smelled fresh bread, the happy scent of her best childhood memories.

Together, they merged with the light.

# The Gold Spinner

In lands far to the north there resided an industrious woman named Frida whose husband died of an illness early in their marriage, leaving her to fend for herself and her only daughter, Hanna.

Frida made her income spinning flax into thread and weaving cloth. As Hanna grew up, Frida taught her how to spin, for it was a family tradition. Yet Hanna showed no aptitude for spinning, or any kind of work. Frida had to nag her to cook, clean, feed the hens, or even light a fire. As Hanna grew into a beautiful girl, Frida worried how her daughter would make her way in the world if she didn't acquire any skills.

One morning, after scolding her daughter for her lack of activity, Frida placed a stool on the straw roof of their cottage and ordered her daughter to sit on it and spin. Frida thought it would shame Hanna into work, as she would be in full view of all their neighbours and the travelers on the road.

Hanna was a cheerful sort, however, and used her time on the roof to enjoy the sunshine and see what everyone was up to from her excellent vantage point.

That day, Prince Birger rode past with a small retinue of men on their way back from a boar hunt. The sun gleamed on Hanna's hair, attracting the Prince's attention. Intrigued by the strange situation of a pretty girl sitting on top of a cottage, with a distaff and spindle lying idly at her feet, he urged his horse from the road. Frida appeared at her door, attracted by the sound of their arrival, but was flustered by the attention of such noble company.

When Prince Birger inquired about Hanna's curious location, Frida answered sarcastically, "She sits there so that everyone can see how clever she is. In fact she's so clever, she can spin gold out of clay and long straw!"

Alas, the Prince was an honest, trusting man and failed to notice Frida's exaggerated tone. The kingdom was in dire need of money after an expensive war, and Birger was at a marriageable age. He was struck by Hanna's beauty and believed that marrying her would solve all his problems.

Hanna came down from her perch on the roof, and

Prince Birger offered to take her with him to the palace to be his consort if she could perform her marvelous feat. Frida turned pale, and realized she would either have to admit she had lied or put her daughter in danger. Before Frida could explain, Hanna agreed to the terms to save her mother from disgrace and punishment.

Mother and daughter had only a few moments to say their goodbyes before Hanna was placed on the Prince's mount and they set off for the palace. During the journey the Prince kept up a lively conversation, but Hanna could barely speak because she was so worried. Birger was sincere and kind, but Hanna had no doubts that a girl of her station would not be acceptable to Birger's family without proof of her wondrous talent.

Indeed it was the case. King Erik and Queen Matilda were less than pleased when their only son arrived home with a sweet peasant girl, whom he claimed could spin gold out of clay and straw. Birger was easily fooled, as his parents had witnessed before, and they suspected Hanna of trying to trap their son into marriage. "She must spin clay and straw into gold for three nights," King Erik said. "The punishment for defrauding the crown is death."

Birger had faith in Hanna, however, and told her so as he left her in a cold, stone tower room with a new distaff and spindle, along with a pail of clay and a bundle of straw. When the door clanged shut, Hanna allowed herself to cry. She looked out of the tower window across the land where her mother's house lay, and wished she was home beside her familiar hearth. When she turned and saw the spindle and distaff, she burst into fresh tears, for they reminded her of her absent mother and the impossible chore.

Suddenly there was an odd grinding noise and an opening appeared in the wall, through which stepped a short, hideous man with a sly smile. Hanna was so taken aback that she stopped crying. He asked why she was in such an agitated state and Hanna told him the truth, for she believed herself doomed.

"Don't worry," he told her. "Take these enchanted gloves. If you wear them while spinning, you will create gold from clay and straw."

Initially Hanna didn't believe him, but she tried them on and they worked as promised. She knew there must be a price.

"I will return for another two nights. If you are able to guess my name, you can keep the gloves and marry the Prince, otherwise I will take you home and you will be my wife."

His leer turned her stomach, but Hanna had little choice and agreed to his terms. He chuckled, bowed, and left through the same magical portal by which he had entered.

Hanna labored for many hours by candlelight until she emptied the pail and no straw remained. She fell into an exhausted sleep.

The next morning, Prince Birger opened the door, eager to check on her. His eyes shone with delight and pride when he saw the gleaming gold. The King and Queen were called immediately and everyone marveled, although privately the King gave orders to double the guard on Hanna's room that night.

Hanna spent the day with Birger, but she was quiet and let him do most of the talking. In her mind, she created long lists of names, desperately trying to guess the identity of the peculiar little man. She became so anxious that she lost her appetite, and after spotting an elderly man begging on the city streets, she put aside some of her food and offered it to him. He blessed her sincerely.

That night, Hanna was locked back in the tower room with two buckets of clay and two bundles of straw. She put on the gloves and set to work right away. Many hours later, as she was finishing, a grinding sound heralded the short man's arrival. She spent another hour listing all the names she knew. He rocked back and forth on his heels and grinned as he exclaimed, "No!" to all her suggestions. Eventually Hanna gave up, and the man left after reminding her of the penalty if she didn't name him correctly the following night.

Prince Birger and his family were full of praise for Hanna the following morning, and by now the King had enough gold to pay off his debts. Another night would procure him enough money to hold a fabulous wedding for Birger and Hanna. While they showered her with compliments, Hanna said little, and everyone praised her humility and modesty.

Unable to eat breakfast, she once again took her food to the street beggar. He noticed her drawn features and red eyes, and asked if there was anything wrong. She outlined the problem, without naming herself as the one in trouble. The man watched her carefully as she recounted her story, and told her she should have a heart for her "friend".

Hanna quickly returned to the palace and raided its library, seeking unusual and exotic names. Later that afternoon, Prince Birger sought her out and, seeing her listless and somber mood, tried to cheer her up.

"My darling," he said — for he was truly in love with her now — "let me relate an odd story that happened today. On our way to the hunt this morning, an old man in the street directed us to a new place to find game. Since it was an area I'd never tried before, I decided we should try our luck.

"It was a longer ride than usual, up a small mountain. During the hunt I became separated from my men. As I searched for them I spied smoke from a fire and followed it. Through the bushes I saw the strangest little man, capering around the fire outside a cave entrance, singing this song:

'Tomorrow a fair beauty I will marry,
For few can find my hidden eyrie,
And no one outside of faerie,
Knows my name is Titteli Ture.'

> His eyes shone with delight and pride when he saw the gleaming gold.

# The Gold Spinner

"At that point I heard the hunter's horn and I followed it back to my companions."

Upon hearing the story, Hanna sat bolt upright, her eyes brimming with hope. That night, the King left her with three buckets of clay and three bundles of straw. Hanna attacked the job with a happy spirit. At one point she laughed when she considered how surprised her mother would be if she could see her working so hard. By the time she had finished, a rosy dawn painted the sky. Then came the familiar grating noise and the man danced out of his portal, grinning from ear to ear.

Hanna restrained her urge to smile and suggested new names. At last impatient, he said, "One final guess, my love, before we depart for our wedding."

She tapped her chin as if deep in thought, then said, "Is it ... Titteli Ture?"

The man's face changed from shades of red to purple while his eyes bulged out.

"Who told you?" he screamed.

"You must leave as we agreed, Titteli Ture!" she ordered. At the sound of his name again, he launched himself at her, fingers clawed out, but she fended him off with her distaff.

All at once they heard a key turning in the lock and both of them froze. With a final curse, Titteli Ture disappeared into his portal just as Prince Birger entered the room.

The marriage of Hanna and Prince Birger was the year's most important event. Afterwards, Frida came to live with her daughter in the palace. Frida was the only person to whom Hanna confessed the story, and as the years passed, mother and daughter would sometimes sit and spin together in the evening. While doing so they would talk, laugh, and at least once sing:

"Tomorrow a fair beauty I will marry,
For few can find my hidden eyrie,
And no one outside of faerie,
Knows my name is Titteli Ture."

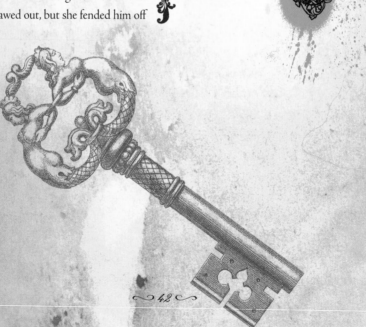

# Vasilisa's Fire

Vasilisa's mother was dying.

Her father ushered little Vasilisa into the sickroom, and left the two of them alone. Haggard with dark rings around her eyes, Vasilisa's mother looked more like a skeleton than a human being. From under the covers she lifted a small, hand-sewn doll with black button eyes, and handed it to her daughter.

"Vasilisa, you are the joy of my life and I'm sorry I'm leaving you so soon. This doll was given to me by my mother. Whenever you need help, give the doll a little food and drink, tell it your troubles, and it will give you advice and aid. Carry it with you always and never show it to anyone." Her mother gasped, as if speaking cost her much. "I cannot be with you but that doll will be my substitute. I love you, my little girl."

At that mother and daughter embraced, and cried. Eventually, her mother kissed Vasilisa on the forehead and sent her out of the room. By nightfall her mother was dead and Vasilisa was inconsolable. She lay in her bed crying and clutching her new doll to her chest. Her grief

was so terrible she thought she too would die. Unable to sleep she decided to follow her mother's advice. Vasilisa went to the kitchen, found a slice of wheat bread and a cup of milk, and set them before the doll.

"Eat and drink, my doll, and listen to my woe. Mama is dead, and I am so alone."

The doll stood and its eyes lit like sparks of fire. It nibbled a morsel of bread and sipped the milk. It gazed at Vasilisa, and said, "Go to bed and lie down, Vasilisa. Close your eyes and I will sing you to sleep. Grief is worse at night, but the morning is wiser than the evening."

Vasilisa carried the doll back to her bedroom and lay down. The doll sang the lullaby her mother used to sing when she was a baby, and Vasilisa was comforted.

During the following months Vasilisa's pain eased, and her father tried to care for her as best he could. He was a wool merchant and had to travel abroad on occasion, so after a time he realized his daughter needed a mother. Plus, he was lonely too.

Many women in the Tsardom tried to catch his

attention for he had a big house, good prospects, and was known to be a kind and charitable man. He became acquainted with a widow called Sveta, who had twin daughters, Nadia and Natasha. Sveta was a plump, charismatic woman who knew how to please a man, and doted on her two girls. The merchant decided she would be a loving wife and the perfect mother for Vasilisa. As soon as they married, Sveta's true character emerged.

She questioned and undermined her husband at every turn, and criticised Vasilisa daily. The only way the merchant found peace was at work, so he spent less time at home, leaving Vasilisa to fend for herself against her stepmother. Sveta always carried bad reports of Vasilisa's behavior to her husband. He knew Vasilisa was not as discourteous and obdurate as Sveta described, but equally he grew weary of being in the middle of their arguments. He took Vasilisa aside one evening and asked her to be patient with her stepmother.

Vasilisa resented being asked to be the reasonable one. "Don't you see, Vasilisa," he said to her, "I trust *you* to make an effort." At that he sighed, and ran his hand through his thinning hair.

So Vasilisa took on the chores Sveta assigned her without complaint. Since Vasilisa was already a pretty girl, Sveta set her jobs that she thought would ruin her good looks, such as weeding the garden in the hot sun, getting up early to set the fires, and scrubbing floors.

She had not reckoned with Vasilisa's doll.

When all of this began, Vasilisa put a piece of cake and a cup of wine before her doll. "Eat and drink, my doll, and listen to my story. Sveta tries to punish me unfairly."

The doll's eyes glowed like fireflies, and it said, "Fret not Vasilisa, go to sleep tonight and I will tend to the chores." In the morning the garden would be free of weeds, the floors sparkling, and the fires roaring hot. The doll even showed Vasilisa how to mix an ointment from herbs to protect her skin from the sun.

As the years passed Vasilisa grew more beautiful, and Sveta hardened more against her. She instructed her daughters to watch Vasilisa at all times and report any misbehavior. Nadia and Natasha were not mean-spirited by nature, but they loved their mother and did as she asked. The twins often felt plain in comparison with their stepsister, and as they grew older they resented more and more how many suitors paid attention to Vasilisa and not to them.

Several men approached Vasilisa's parents for permission to court her, but Sveta insisted that the twins must marry first. The girls came to the same opinion as their mother: Vasilisa would have to go.

Throughout this period Vasilisa was frequently miserable and lonely for it was difficult to remain strong in the face of those who demonstrated their dislike daily. Her one source of happiness was the doll she carried in

> The girls came to the same opinion as their mother: Vasilisa would have to go.

her pocket, and she often blessed her mother for leaving her such a gift.

One day Vasilisa's father announced that he had to leave on a long, arduous journey to a distant Tsardom, which would take him many months. He said goodbye to his family, and asked them to pray for his safety while he was gone.

Vasilisa knew she was the one that needed the prayers.

A couple of weeks after he departed, Nadia and Natasha banged into Vasilisa's bedroom and ordered her to pack all her belongings. She discovered Sveta had sold the house and all its furniture and had bought a small cottage next to the dark woods, a place notorious for bandits and fierce creatures. They were leaving that afternoon. Vasilisa reached into her pocket and touched the doll for reassurance, and put together a small trunk of clothes.

In the new house Vasilisa was given a tiny attic room, and forced to do all the work. Even with the help of the doll she was weary every evening; more so from the constant complaints from Sveta and the twins.

Her stepmother found constant excuses to send Vasilisa into the forest on errands. One day it was to collect blackberries and another day to pick mushrooms. Each time Vasilisa consulted her doll for advice so she could complete her job and travel in and out of the forest without injury. In particular, she took care to avoid the

hut of Baba Yaga, a terrifying witch who was reputed to eat those who wandered into her territory. Nadia and Natasha loved to relate blood-curdling stories about the witch to frighten Vasilisa each time Sveta sent her into the forest.

One evening Vasilisa overheard Sveta and her daughters whispering together, a sure sign they were plotting. Vasilisa ensured she had food and drink on her in case she needed to confer with her doll. Later, Sveta instructed Nadia to crochet a lace collar, Natasha to knit a sock, and Vasilisa to spin a basket of flax. She put out all the fires and lights and left a single candle burning in their room, and retired to bed. The girls worked for several hours, until Nadia got up to adjust the candle wick, and snuffed out the flame.

"What shall we do?" asked Natasha, "We have no way to light the candle."

"I know," said Nadia, "Vasilisa can go to Baba Yaga's hut and ask the witch for a light."

Vasilisa tried to argue with her stepsisters, but they bundled her out of the door, and closed it against her. "Don't return unless you come back with a flame from Baba Yaga's house," they warned her.

Vasilisa sat down on the doorstep, shivering at the thought of deliberately seeking out the witch. She gave her doll food and drink, and in the darkness its eyes were tiny moons. Vasilisa explained her problem to the doll.

"Fear not, Vasilisa," it said, "I will direct you to the

> Vasilisa sat down on the doorstep, shivering at the thought of deliberately seeking out the witch.

witch's house, and you will come to no harm. Baba Yaga is fearsome, but you will survive if you abide by her rules."

Vasilisa returned the doll to her pocket, and ventured into the wild forest. The doll tugged on her skirt on the right if that was the direction she needed to go, or on the left if that was the best route.

At one point a rider dressed in white galloped by riding a snow-white horse wearing a white harness. The night softened into early dawn. A few hours later a rider with a red face wearing scarlet clothing and riding a ruby-red horse cantered past, and the sun appeared over the horizon. During the day Vasilisa got lost, for her doll was no longer animated and she had no provisions to feed it. All day Vasilisa continued in the direction the doll last indicated and hoped for the best.

Finally, as evening eased into night, she came to a house she knew must be the witch's. It was a hut held aloft by giant chicken legs, standing in a green lawn. It was protected by a fence made entirely of huge bones, which were topped with human skulls. Its bone gate had hinges fashioned from human feet, and its lock was a jawbone with sharpened teeth. Vasilisa trembled at the gruesome sight.

At that moment she heard thundering hooves. A rider with a coal-black face, riding a black steed, trotted up to the gate, and disappeared as if they had merged with the ground. In that instant night descended.

Immediately, fire erupted inside the skulls on the fence. The flames flickered in their eye sockets and lit up the entire area. The row of skulls grinned ghoulishly at Vasilisa, as if they guessed her fate and it amused them.

Then the tree branches started to thrash about and their trunks groaned as Baba Yaga appeared. She was riding in her giant iron mortar, which she directed with a pestle. She swept away her trail with a broom. The witch was tall and lanky, and her long grey hair streamed behind her in braids woven with the finger bones and claws of many creatures.

Her vehicle hovered before her gate, and she called out "Little House, little House, Stand as your mother placed you, Turn your back to the forest, And your face to me!"

The house creaked and swivelled, and its legs slowly bent until it rested on the ground.

Baba Yaga sniffed and her nose twitched. She leaned far out of her mortar until her hatchet face was close to Vasilisa's. "A girl!" she cried. "And just in time for supper!"

Vasilisa curtsied low, and tried to still her shaking. "My name is Vasilisa, Grandmother. I have been sent by my stepsisters to ask for fire for there is none in my stepmother's house."

"Ha! I know those women," the witch said, and she cackled. "There's nothing free in the wide world, my dear, especially not a witch's fire. If you complete some tasks to my satisfaction I will give you fire. If not..." she licked her

> **Its bone gate had hinges fashioned from human feet, and its lock was a jawbone with sharpened teeth.**

lips, "You'll be in my cooking pot."

Vasilisa nearly fled at that prospect, but she remembered what her doll told her, and she nodded in agreement to the terms.

Baba Yaga straightened, faced her gate and shouted, "Ho! Ye, my solid lock, unlock! Ho! Ye, my stout gate, open!" The lock snapped open, and the gate swung wide. Baba Yaga rode in whistling. Vasilisa followed reluctantly. Behind her the gate closed and the lock clicked shut.

They entered the witch's hut, festooned with garlands of bones and bundles of herbs, and stocked with shelves of potions. There were four skulls with gleaming eyes, one in each corner, lighting the room. Baba Yaga tipped herself into large armchair and crossed her bony ankles in front of the potbellied stove. "Take the meat from the oven, make me a meal, and set it on the table."

Vasilisa scurried to please the witch. There was enough cooked meat for three giants. She also found a jug of red wine, bread, and she made cabbage soup. Baba Yaga pulled up to the table and attacked the meal with gusto, slurping and chomping. Afterwards she let out a deafening burp. All that remained for Vasilisa was a drip of soup, a crust of bread, and a cube of bacon.

The old witch's eyelids began to droop with drowsiness. She dropped into her bed by the stove, and said to Vasilisa: "Tomorrow, after I leave, you will clean the yard, sweep the floors, and cook my supper. Also, take a quarter of a measure of wheat from the storehouse, and remove all the black grains and the wild peas. If this is not all done by the time I return, *you* will be my meal!"

Presently, Baba Yaga began to snore. Vasilisa waited a little longer, went into a corner, removed the doll from her pocket, and fed it bread and a little cabbage soup. Its eyes gleamed like stars. Vasilisa opened her mouth to speak but instead burst into tears, overcome by the day's events. In between sniffs and snuffles she related the witch's demands to the doll.

"Go to sleep, kind Vasilisa," it replied, "The morning is wiser than the evening." Feeling better, Vasilisa curled up in the armchair and fell into an exhausted sleep.

She woke up to hear the witch already outside, whistling cheerfully. She looked out the window just as the scarlet horseman arrived at the gate and disappeared, and dawn arrived.

Baba Yaga leaped into her huge mortar as it lifted off the ground. Stormy winds whipped around her. She yelled at the gate, "Ho! Ye, my solid lock, unlock! Ho! Ye, my stout gate, open!" The lock and the gate opened, and she sped away in the mortar, steering with the pestle, and sweeping her path behind her with the broom.

With a shock, Vasilisa suddenly remembered all the work she had to complete before the witch's return. She picked up a broom to start, but noticed the floors were swept, the yard outside was clean, and when she checked on the wheat she discovered the doll finishing the job of separating it.

She ran to the doll and hugged it to her chest. "Thank you, dearest doll! Now all I have to do is prepare the witch's supper."

"You are welcome, Vasilisa. Rest today and cook well later."

By the time the black horseman arrived, and the bending of the trees announced Baba Yaga's arrival, Vasilisa had created a wonderful feast for the witch. The crone muttered and grumbled when she checked the young girl's work, but she could find no fault. She munched and crunched on the bones of her meal. Afterwards she clapped her hands three times, and shouted: "Ho! my faithful servants! Friends of my heart! Haste and grind my wheat!" Three pairs of disembodied hands appeared, seized the wheat, and carried it away. Vasilisa bit her lip to stop from crying out in surprise.

Baba Yaga flopped down in her bed and glared at the girl. "You think you're a clever one, eh? Tomorrow you will repeat today's chores, *and* take from my storehouse a half-measure of poppy seeds and clean them one by one. Someone mixed earth with them to do me a mischief, not that he's alive any more." She cackled. "Nor will you be if you don't complete these jobs properly!" She turned to the wall, and soon her snores were shaking the bed.

Vasilisa went into a corner of the room and fed her doll some cheese and milk, and its eyes became like twin candle flames. She explained what needed to be done, and the doll assured her everything would be ready in the morning. Vasilisa lay down to sleep, ever grateful for the doll her mother left her.

The following morning Baba Yaga set off flying and Vasilisa discovered the doll had been true to its word. All the chores were complete, and even the poppy seeds had been polished and sorted. She thanked the doll profusely, and it climbed into her pocket and went limp. Vasilisa spent the day readying a great banquet for the witch, cooking enough for a dozen men.

When she heard the forest groaning at the witch's passage, she readied herself for Baba Yaga's inspection. Once again the witch could raise no complaint. She sat down to her meal in a foul temper, and chewed through all the dishes without leaving a crumb. After, she clapped and called out, "Ho! my trusty servants! Friends of my soul! Haste and press the oil out of my poppy seeds!" The three pairs of disembodied hands appeared, seized the measure of poppy seeds, and carried it away.

The old witch stared at Vasilisa suspiciously for a long time, grinding her teeth. Vasilisa maintained her composure despite her anxiety. Eventually the witch snapped, "Explain how you accomplished all the tasks I set you? Tell me!"

The witch's stare was so compelling that Vasilisa

almost blurted out the explanation about the little doll. She checked herself in time, but also understood that the witch would recognize a lie. She answered: "The blessing of my dead mother protects and helps me."

Baba Yaga leaped up, and shrieked: "Get out of my house this instant! No one who bears a blessing is welcome across my threshold!"

Vasilisa did not need to be told twice. She ran outside, and heard the old witch shouting to the lock and the gate, which opened at her command. Baba Yaga leaned out of her window, and flung one of the skulls with burning eyes at Vasilisa. "There," she howled, "Is the fire for your stepmother's daughters. Shame on them for sending you to me. I have honored our agreement. *May they enjoy the warmth this fire brings!*"

Vasilisa picked up the skull, and placed it on the end of a stick. She darted into the forest, finding her path by the skull's glowing eyes. At dawn, the light in the skull dimmed, just as she spotted the outline of her stepmother's house.

Vasilisa had been gone for days, so she imagined the women had by now started a fire in the house. She was about to throw the skull into the hedge, but it spoke in a clacking voice, "Do not throw me away, Vasilisa! Bring me to your stepsisters as they ordered."

At this she noticed there was no light glinting through the windows, so she carried the skull to the house. As she

approached the fire in the eyes burned bright again.

For the first time ever Sveta welcomed her, and Nadia and Natasha embraced her.

"Thank heavens you returned!" exclaimed Sveta. "Since you left no fire will burn in our house!"

They related how no spark would spring from flint striking steel, and any fire taken into the house from a neighbor's would extinguish as soon as it crossed their doorway. They had been unable to light candles or fires, stay warm, or cook food. They had been cold and living in darkness while Vasilisa was away.

They were delighted that the witch's fire continued to burn after Vasilisa carried it into the house. Sveta grabbed the skull from Vasilisa and brought it into the parlor. Nadia placed a candlestick on the table, and Natasha set the skull upon it.

They admired it, while Vasilisa hung back, for she thought the glowing skull was an eerie sight.

The eyes of the skull slowly began to burn hotter, like red coals. Sveta, Nadia, and Natasha stepped back, alarmed. The skull's fire blazed hot as a furnace, and a jet of flames blasted from the eyes and engulfed Sveta. She screeched in agony and lit up like a bonfire. Nadia and Natasha attempted to flee but the skull turned to follow their path, and the streams of fire shot at them too. Within seconds they were screaming columns of flame.

As quickly as they caught fire, they were reduced to

> The skull's fire blazed hot as a furnace, and a jet of flames blasted from the eyes and engulfed Sveta.

three scorch marks and a pile of ashes.

Vasilisa was rooted at the doorway, shocked and sickened. It had happened so quickly she had been unable to do anything.

The skull turned to gaze at her, but the light began to fade. The fire disappeared, and the skull collapsed into a pile of fine, white powder.

Vasilisa sat down in a chair with a thump. Nothing moved in the silent house. She was alone for the first time. She removed the doll from her pocket, and set before it dried beef and a cup of beer. "Eat and drink, my doll, and listen to my question. Now Sveta and the twins are dead, what shall be my direction?"

The doll's eyes shone like the sun.

"Your father will return soon, Vasilisa, but now is the time to determine your own fortune. You have this house, and your skills. And I will always be with you to offer advice. Be fearless and seize your destiny."

Vasilisa smiled at the doll, and for the first time dreamed of what *she* would like to do.

# Molly Whupple

Molly Whupple was the youngest of a family of fifteen children, and braver than all of them put together. Her brothers and sisters were blonde and blue-eyed, but Molly had hair black as a raven's wing, and eyes green as an oak leaf. From the age of three she claimed to understand the babble of the water sprites in the creek, and played with pixies in the long grass. She was always inventing songs and games, and had a knack for mischief. Inevitably, she roped in her two older sisters, Sally and Edith.

Their parents were busy from dawn to dusk, and they expected their children to behave and help with chores. Molly constantly distracted the others, which annoyed their father in particular. Nothing Molly did ever pleased him.

During a lean winter when food was scarce and the family shivered in their freezing house, Molly woke one night to hear whispers between her mother and father in the darkness.

"They're girls," her father said, "and we have others."

Her mother sobbed. Molly couldn't hear what else was said, but she knew the sound of a plot being hatched.

The next day their father ordered Sally, Edith, and Molly to dress warmly and accompany him to the forest to collect holly to sell in the market. Their mother hugged them with tears in her eyes. While no one was watching, Molly stole withered apples and hard cheese from the table and stuffed them into her pockets.

They walked into the forest for a long time, until even Molly couldn't recognize where they where. Snow drifted down steadily. When they came to an area thick with holly bushes their father gave Sally a small knife to cut the branches, and told the girls he was going to another patch of holly and would collect them on the way back.

Molly followed him, but he noticed and brought her back to her sisters. He warned Sally and Edith that if Molly didn't stay with them then none of them would have supper that evening.

When he left again, Molly's sisters held her so she couldn't pursue him.

# Molly Whupple

Several hours later the shadows between the trees thickened. Sally and Edith had cut a stack of holly branches. Molly, perched on top a boulder, watched them, sulking. "He's not coming back," she said, and blew on the tips of her fingers, which poked through her threadbare mittens.

"He's our dad," Sally said. "Of course he'll return."

Edith placed her hands under her armpits, and stamped her feet to keep warm. Worry wrinkles creased her forehead. "Where did you get that idea, Molly?"

"An owl hooted it to me last night."

"Ignore her, Edith," said Sally, for she could see Edith puckering up to cry.

"I'm hungry!" wailed Edith.

In the distance they heard the call of a wolverine. Edith's mouth snapped shut. The three girls glanced at each other. It had been a hard winter.

"We have to go," Molly said, and jumped down from the rock.

Sally began to protest: "Father said-"

"Do you remember how long it took to get here? If we don't set off for home now we'll get lost in the darkness. Here, have some apple and cheese."

The three girls, led by Molly, tried to find the path home, but the snow had covered their tracks. Twilight descended and the temperature plummeted. Sally held Edith close to her for warmth when they stopped to assess their situation.

"Give me the knife, Sally," Molly ordered. Sally handed it over, too tired and cold to argue.

Molly hummed a little tune and looked about until she saw a thicket of hazel. She cut off a thin branch and stripped the twigs until she had a divining rod.

"Hazel stick, do your trick, point and lead, to bed and bread," she sang.

The stick spun Molly about and twitched in a direction. "Come on!" Molly said, her voice high and excited. Sally and Edith trudged after their younger sister.

The girls were exhausted and frozen when they spotted a light winking through the trees. They found their way to a huge two-story wooden house, with smoke billowing from the chimney. The doorway and windows were twice the normal size, but the sisters were too tired to wonder at it.

Sally banged on the door.

A tall, raw-boned woman with a long face answered. A blast of heat washed over the girls.

"Please, may we have shelter for the night?" Sally asked through chapped lips. "We're lost, and hungry."

The woman looked about as if checking for someone. "You can't stop here. My husband's a giant, and he might eat the likes of you."

The three girls pleaded for a short rest and a little to eat. The night was so cruel and the girls so persistent that the woman relented.

Her name was Greta, and she sat the sisters in front of

the large fireplace, and fed them goats' milk and a slice of meat pie each.

As they licked the crumbs from their fingers, they felt thumping steps approach the house.

The door banged open and a giant stood in the doorway carrying the carcass of a deer. His busy eyebrows curved down together as he scowled.

"Fe fi fo fum, I smell the flesh of earthly ones!" he bellowed.

"Stop that nonsense, Wil," Greta said. "These three girls are Sally, Edith, and Molly, and they were perishing outside. They'll be off at first light, right girls?"

They nodded silently, in awe of the giant.

He sat at the table, scowling. His wife disappeared into a back room with the deer, and returned hauling a huge platter of cooked meats that she set down in front of him. He attacked it with enthusiasm. Soon only a pile of bones remained, which he proceeded to crack open with his teeth to suck out the marrow. All the time he glared at the three girls.

After he'd eaten, Greta ushered the girls upstairs, into a darkened bedroom. Inside was a huge bed in which three girls lay asleep. Whispering, Greta told Sally, Edith and Molly that these were their triplets. Greta lifted the blankets at the bottom of the bed, and the sisters crawled in. The bed was so large that their feet didn't touch those of the triplets.

The giant appeared in the doorway. He laid a noose of gold links around his daughters' necks. Then he kissed their foreheads.

He handed nooses of rough horse hair to Molly and her sisters. "Wear these," he said gruffly. Sally and Edith were practically asleep, and they did so without complaint. The giant noticed Molly's suspicion. "It's to keep you safe," he explained. "The cold weather brings out bandits. We'll know if they try to steal you away." Molly put on the noose and lay back. Greta and the giant left the room.

Molly didn't fall asleep despite her exhaustion. As soon as everyone was snoozing she swapped the loops of horse hair around her and her sisters' necks with the rings of gold chains from the triplets. She lay back, wide awake, waiting.

Presently, the floorboards creaked outside her room. Molly half shut her eyelids. The giant's hand reached into the room and grabbed the ropes of horse hair. With a sudden, vicious yank, he pulled the ropes to him. The nooses tightened immediately around the triplets' necks, cutting off all sound.

They fell in a pile on the ground. The giant lifted a huge club and beat the girls to death. Molly clamped her hands over her mouth, because the crack of bone and the splatter of blood made her want to scream. She gagged, but remained silent. Moments later the giant left the room.

Molly lay shaking in the bed until she heard the rattle

**Molly clamped her hands over her mouth, because the crack of bone and the splatter of blood made her want to scream.**

of the giant's snores next door. Quietly, she woke Sally and Edith, and told them they were leaving. Molly was so insistent, and they were so scared of the giant, that they obeyed her without protest. They tiptoed downstairs, and Molly filled all their pockets with food. They let themselves out of the house. It wasn't yet dawn, but the skies were clear, and there was no snow. The girls noticed a trail and followed it out until they came to a road. Then they ran as fast as they could for as long as they could. By the time it was bright they had arrived at the castle of Duke Wendell.

The girls were taken to the duke and Molly related the story. The giant was well known to everyone as he terrorized the region.

The duke was impressed with Molly's fortitude and cleverness. He ordered that the girls be given baths, new clothes, and to join the duke and his family for a meal. The duke was a widower with three sons: Frederick, Oswald, and Harald. Sally and Edith took an instant liking to the oldest two. Molly rolled her eyes at her sisters, and concentrated on eating.

Several days later the duke called Molly into his private study. "Do you want me to send a message to your parents?" he asked.

"Never!" Molly said vehemently. "We'll make our own fortune now."

The duke took a moment to appraise Molly. "Your sister Sally has been spending a lot of time with my oldest son, Frederick."

Molly crossed her arms. "She's not good enough for him?"

The duke laughed. "Maybe she would be... if you stole the giant's sword. It has a magic blade, which cuts through all armor and kills anyone from the tiniest scratch. It makes him a terrible foe to defeat."

"I'll think about it," she said.

Immediately, Molly searched out Sally, and found her embroidering Frederick's name on a piece of linen cloth.

"Do you like him?" Molly asked.

Sally blushed, but spent an hour detailing to Molly all of Frederick's best traits, from his up-turned nose to his ability at horse-riding.

Molly sighed, shook her head, and agreed to the duke's bargain. She consulted a map of the terrain, then dressed herself warmly in knee-high boots, leather pants, and a tightly-fitted coat. The clothes belonged to the duke's youngest son Harald, and he spotted her slipping on a heavy wool cape as she prepared to leave.

He stared at her and Molly glared. "If you laugh, or tell my sisters what I'm doing, I'll punch you." Molly had brawled with her brothers on many occasions and knew the easiest ways to hurt a boy.

Harald raised an eyebrow at her threat, and smiled. "You look fetching."

She hit him on the arm as she passed by.

*She noticed three fresh grave mounds, stark against the snow, at the back of the house.*

Molly cut another divining rod to lead her back to the giant's house, and once there she spent some time hiding in a nearby tree observing Greta and the giant's routine. She noticed three fresh grave mounds, stark against the snow, at the back of the house. Molly thought about the three girls, dead because the giant tried to murder her and her sisters. Her lips compressed in a thin, determined line.

Late in the afternoon, when Greta was busy in the stables and the giant left, hefting a huge club over his shoulder, Molly snuck into the house, and quickly searched the rooms for the sword. Finally, in the giant's bedroom, she discovered it hanging over the bed. At that moment the giant returned, and Molly retired to the girls' bedroom. The floor had been scrubbed but the bloodstains were still visible. She slipped under the bed and hid for the rest of the evening until Greta and the giant retired.

Molly waited many hours until the couple were deep asleep before she crept into the room. She had to stand on the edge of the bed frame to reach the sword. Luckily, it was fashioned for a human, not a giant, so she was able to lift it.

As she hit the first step of the staircase it let out a tremendous squeak. The giant woke up instantly, and roared.

Molly fled down the stairs and out of the house with the sword strapped to her back. Behind her were the thundering steps of the giant. Molly had mapped out her return route and she would cross a massive river, flowing swift with icy water.

She got to the edge of its frozen bank, and plucked a hair from her head.

"Water Sprite, With your might, Let me cross, A One Hair Bridge."

She threw her hair to the ground. It speared into the mud, and grew to span the water. Molly took a deep breath and ran nimbly over the one hair bridge. When she reached the far side, she saw the giant skid to a halt at the water's edge. It wouldn't take his weight. He struck the ground with his club in fury. There were no other bridges for miles around. Molly ran to a nearby clearing where she had told the duke to leave her a horse.

When she arrived she found Harald on another horse waiting for her.

"Father never expected you to survive," Harald said as she climbed onto her horse.

"He'd better honor his bargain."

"Oh he will. That sword was my grandfather's. He'll be overjoyed to have it back."

Sure enough, the duke was thrilled to have such a powerful weapon returned to his family. With his blessing, Sally and Frederick were engaged to be married.

Several weeks later the duke found Molly playing a game of chess with Harald in a room while Sally talked of wedding plans with Fredrick. Edith and Oswald laughed in a corner as they tried to compose a song for a lute. The duke beckoned to Molly and they went for a chat in the garden.

"Edith and Oswald seem rather attached," the duke began. Molly nodded. The two of them were always together. Their feelings were obvious to all the gossips in the castle. "Weddings are expensive..." he continued.

Molly cocked her head at him. "Let me guess, the giant has a treasure."

"He has stolen enough gold for at least two grand weddings...."

Later, Harald found Molly dressed to leave on an adventure. "I'll accompany you," he said.

"No! This is my responsibility. The only person who gets hurt if I fail is me."

Harald tried to argue with her, but she refused to listen. In the end she agreed that he could meet her that night with the horses at the same location as before.

Molly returned to the giant's house and spied on him and his wife. They seemed more vigilant, and it was several hours before Molly had an opportunity. She snuck into the house and headed straight to the giant's bedroom. In her previous search she had not discovered the gold, so she was sure it must be in that room.

She had just located the large bag of coins under the giant's pillow when the front door banged. Molly slid under the giant's bed for he went straight to the bedroom complaining to his wife of a fever. For the rest of the evening he lay in bed, the mattress bowed close to Molly's nose, and he coughed, sneezed, and complained.

During the dead of night, nearly deafened by the giant's congested snoring, Molly slunk out from under the bed. With agonizing slowness, she inched the bag of coins from under the pillow of the slumbering giant.

This time she remembered the creaking top step, but before she got there she tripped over one of the giant's shoes. He opened his eyes and spotted her instantly.

"You again!" he stormed, and jumped up.

Molly dashed down the stairs, out the house, and behind her came the roaring and rumbling of the giant. This time the river was even wider and faster due to melting snows, and she tugged a hair from her head to create a one hair bridge.

She was nearly across the river, when the giant lumbered up to the other side. This time he pulled the hair out of the mud on his side of the river. He whipped it hard and Molly was flung off the hair and into the mud on the far side. He screamed when he saw Molly pick herself up, covered in filth, and wave at him.

When she squelched up to Harald some time later he nearly fell off his horse laughing at her. She didn't speak to him the whole way back to the castle.

True to his word, the duke announced the engagement of Edith and Oswald, and Molly spent much of the subsequent months trying to avoid both her sisters and their endless discussions about dresses, invitations, and recipes for elaborate wedding dishes.

In the early summer, Sally and Frederick were married, and Molly was forced into a silk dress, the color of emerald, for the occasion. After the pomp and ceremony, she and Harald talked for much of the meal about chess strategies and only joined in with the dancing when Sally forced both of them onto the floor. Molly discovered she liked it more than she expected.

A week later she was in the castle library reading a story of magic and adventure when the duke came in and closed the door behind him. She knew him well enough to realize that his serious expression warned of trouble for her.

"Harald has spoken to me about you," he said.

Molly's cheeks got a little hot. "Do you want me to stop beating him at chess?"

"Harald was promised to the priesthood when he was a child. This autumn he will be leaving to begin his studies."

Molly wondered if all the air had suddenly departed the room. "Oh," was all she could say.

"He doesn't want to go."

A smile tugged at Molly's lips. "Oh."

"He cannot easily withdraw. I must give the cardinal a gift in compensation."

She sighed. "And the giant possesses such a gift?"

"You're a clever girl Molly. It's a gold ring the giant wears at all times. It's a relic of the patron saint of the cardinal. He will release Harald from his promise for such a venerated item."

"You can't tell Harald why I am doing this."

The duke nodded, and left Molly to plot.

Two days later Molly left the castle before dawn.

This time she crept into the house and dosed the giant's ale with a sleeping draught, before hiding under his bed. She had with her a small pat of butter. When the giant and his wife's snores shook the bedroom later, Molly slowly smeared butter on the ring on the giant's pinkie finger and eased it off. Just as she dropped the ring into her pocket the giant woke up, seized her by the wrist, and dangled her above the floor.

"Now I've caught you, Molly! What should I do with you?"

Quick as a whip, Molly answered, "Tie me up in a sack and hang me on a peg. Fetch your club from the shed and beat me to death."

"That's a very good plan!"

The giant dragged Molly down the steps and Greta followed them. He had Greta get a burlap sack, threw Molly into it, and hung her from a peg. He stamped out of the house to find his club.

As soon as the giant was out of the door Molly sighed loudly. "Oh, if only you could see what I see."

Greta snapped, "It's a potato sack! There's nothing in there except you."

Molly sang out again. "Oh, if only you could see what I see."

Greta began to wonder if Molly had managed to

*She was nearly across the river, when the giant lumbered up to the other side.*

enchant the sack in some fashion. "Tell me what you can see," she begged.

"I can't, you must see for yourself. It's too marvelous!"

Overcome with curiosity, Greta untied the bag and pulled Molly out. She stuck her head in. "I can't see anything!" she complained.

"Lean in further," Molly said, and as Greta did so, Molly pushed her into the sack and knotted it closed again. Greta made a big commotion, and Molly hid behind the door.

The giant came running into the room and hit the bag with his club. His wife screeched, "It's me, you fool!" But Molly had already run out the door and into the cover of night. There was much cursing and crashing behind her, and it sounded like the husband and wife were engaged in a furious fight.

By the time she reached the river, Molly could hear the giant far behind her, which was just as well as the river was much less wide and fierce. She summoned her one hair bridge and arrived at the clearing.

Harald was waiting, and when he saw her an expression of relief crossed his features. Molly climbed onto her horse, and they began their long journey back to the castle.

"Did you get what you wanted?" he asked as they rode back under a clear sky.

She reached over and put the ring on his finger.

# Little Red Hood

In a village bordering a vast forest lived a seamstress named Nadine and her young daughter, Charlotte. Nadine was highly skilled with her needle and all the fashionable ladies in the area sought her out. She had learned her craft from her own mother, who lived in a cottage in the middle of the forest. Charlotte always had beautiful clothes because her mother and grandmother were constantly making her something new to wear.

Most of all, Charlotte loved a red-hooded cape her grandmother had sewn for her. It was embroidered with images of fairies and flowers, and Charlotte wore it so often everyone in the town could recognize her immediately. Some of the townsfolk called her Little Red Hood as a nickname.

One day Nadine presented her daughter with a new cloak. It was the color of a fresh green meadow, had a secret pocket on the inside, and was edged with a silk ribbon. "You'll be the envy of everyone," Nadine told her daughter when Charlotte modeled it for her. "That red cape is too short and a bit worn now."

Charlotte thanked her mother, but she hung the cloak at the back of her closet. For the following week every time she left the house in her red cloak her mother would exclaim, "Why are you wearing that old thing? Put on your new one instead." Charlotte felt obliged to change it to keep her mother happy, but she didn't like how no one knew who she was on sight or that people commented on how much she had grown up.

A few days later Nadine was working hard on a new order when she received word from her good friend Poppy that Nadine's mother was unwell. Poppy was a laundress who washed clothes in the forest river, and as a favor Poppy often dropped by to check on Nadine's mother.

Nadine called Charlotte into her workshop. Poppy was drinking a cup of tea while Nadine cut cloth with scissors. As usual she wore a small cushion on her wrist studded with pins.

"I need you to visit your grandmother tomorrow," Nadine told Charlotte, without taking her eyes off the

pattern she was cutting. "Bring her a pail of milk and I'll bake her bread in the morning."

Poppy laughed, "Milk! For *your mother?*"

Nadine considered, and amended, "Take a flask of wine instead."

The following day Charlotte put on her red cloak and placed the wine and bread in a wicker basket. When she said goodbye to her mother Nadine noticed the cloak, and smiled. "Don't tell her I made you a new one." Nadine kissed her daughter on her forehead and instructed her to take the shortest, safest route to the house.

Charlotte swung her basket cheerfully as she strolled through the village, and enjoyed how many people called out "Hello Little Red Hood!" to her. It was a mild day, and Charlotte enjoyed the walk.

Outside the village she came to a crossroads. If she continued straight ahead she would be at her grandmother's house in short order, but if she took the left turn she would pass by a pasture full of flowers. Charlotte decided to take the longer, prettier path that wended this way and that way through the forest. "*I'll gather flowers to cheer Granny up*", Charlotte thought.

A short time later she passed woodsmen felling trees and she waved at them. "Little Red Hood!" they called to her. One of them whistled at her in admiration, and she stuck her nose in the air to indicate her disapproval. The men burst out laughing, and she hurried her step.

A short time later she saw a man lazing against the stump of a tree watching the road. She nodded to him politely. He leaped up in an agile, easy manner, and bowed with his hat in hand.

"Good day pretty maid," he said, in a deep, gruff voice, "where are you off to?"

Charlotte slowed but kept walking. "Good day sir. I'm visiting my sick grandmother."

The man's eyes were almost orange under the shade of the trees, and he was altogether the hairiest fellow Charlotte had ever seen.

"Good girls like you should beware of being in the forest alone," he said, and his voice dropped to almost a growl.

Behind her came the creaking, crashing sound of a tree falling. "You are never alone in the forest," Charlotte replied, something her grandmother often said. "With one cry I could summon a group of woodsmen with axes."

"Aye, you could. But maybe they would like to chop up a girl like you." The man stepped closer and sniffed in a way that reminded Charlotte of a dog.

"That's if they could catch me. I'm fast, and besides, I can take care of myself."

"Can you, my dear," he said, and moved even closer.

"Oh yes, I'm skilled with a knife."

The man looked down and noticed that Charlotte had pulled a dagger from under her cloak and pointed it directly at his belly.

His laugh was a harsh bark. "Aren't you a delicious surprise," he said.

Charlotte tightened the grip on the dagger and loosened her arm holding the basket. "My grandmother knows all about the forest, and she taught me well."

The man raised his nose as if scenting something. "Does she, my sweet? I would like to meet her sometime. To discuss the ways of the wild."

"Do you know this song?" Charlotte sang a ditty:

*Hie away all that's evil,*
*Under the greenwood tree*
*Hie away all that's evil*
*Make this path safe*
*for me.*

At those words the man's face twisted into a grimace and he walked backwards from her into the forest. He snapped at the air as if trying to attack something invisible. Before he disappeared his eyes glowed yellow and he yelled, "Watch your step, young miss!"

Charlotte kept her dagger in her hand for the next section of forest path, until the trees thinned out and revealed a pasture of lush grass and tall nodding flowers. The sun was shining and Charlotte hummed to herself as she picked a bouquet of sweet-smelling blooms.

After a while she noticed the sun was dipping down past the tree line, and she hurried back to the trail. It was darker now, so she picked up her pace until she could see the familiar outline of her grandmother's cottage.

Charlotte knocked on the door and called out "Granny, it's Lottie," which was her grandmother's pet name for Charlotte.

She thought she heard a noise like a stool falling over, but a feeble voice croaked, "Dear Lottie, come in. I'm too ill to rise from my bed."

Alarmed, Charlotte lifted the latch on the door and walked in. The shutters on the windows were fastened shut, and other than the fire there was little light in the large room. Her Granny had a bed on the right-hand side, heaped with pillows and blankets. Charlotte could barely detect the gleam of her grandmother's eyes under her floppy white nightcap.

"How are you feeling, Granny?" Charlotte asked.

"I just had something to eat, so that perked me up."

Charlotte set her basket down on the kitchen table, and took off her cloak. "Your voice is terribly rough, shall I pour you some wine? Mama gave me a flask and a loaf of bread for you."

Her Granny coughed. "No sweet child, I have a cup of wine poured. Why don't you take a sip? You must be parched. It's there on the dresser."

Charlotte could make out the large earthenware mug sitting on the oak dresser. She was surprised. Her grandmother always drank wine from a delicate glass goblet she'd inherited from her mother.

Charlotte picked up the cup but immediately

> Charlotte could barely detect the gleam of her grandmother's eyes under her floppy white nightcap.

wrinkled her nose. "It smells sour, Granny."

"I can smell its aroma from here, and it makes my mouth water. Have a taste."

"What a good nose you have, Granny, but you must be very sick indeed for this doesn't smell of wine at all."

"Don't refuse your Granny's hospitality. Drink!"

Just then she felt her Granny's big ginger cat, Tom, brush against her legs. She reached down to scratch his ears, and he looked up at her with bright, emerald eyes. A voice purred, "It's blood, not wine."

"Throw a shoe at that noisy cat," her Granny growled.

Charlotte recoiled from Tom, but she was also startled at her Granny's words. She doted on the animal.

"What good hearing you have, Granny, he hardly made a sound."

"Ignore the beast, and drink! I'll deal with him later."

Charlotte raised the cup to her lips and pretended to take a small sip. This close the contents smelled like a butcher's shop, and her stomach roiled. She noticed the cup was lukewarm, and its sides were sticky. She almost gagged, but instead said, "Thank you Granny."

"Bring me the cup, and let me look upon you."

Charlotte moved to her grandmother's bedside, and handed her the cup. Her Granny's hands brushed her, and she was struck at how hairy they were.

"Your hands are so hairy, Granny, I never noticed before," Charlotte was never one for censoring any

thought before she spoke it, something Nadine pointed out often.

"It happens with old age, my love." Granny gulped back the wine with a loud slurping. She even seemed to lick the cup afterwards.

Charlotte's grandmother was finicky about proper table manners so that was unusual. Her Granny placed the cup on the bedside shelf, and in the dim light her eyes glowed orange with pleasure.

"Your eyes..." Charlotte trailed off, for it struck her that perhaps she should not continue that thought out loud, for once.

"Are wide in anticipation of seeing you properly. Come closer, for they are weak."

As Charlotte leaned in, she smelled a musk that she associated with damp dog's fur after it had run through a forest, chasing prey. Her Granny smiled, wide, far too wide, and with far too many sharp teeth.

"Come close and kiss your Granny," she said, her voice the rasp of sandpaper. She clamped a hairy hand on Charlotte's wrist, and dragged her to the bed.

"You're not my grandmother!" cried Charlotte.

It was the man from the forest but he was more wolf than man now.

"She didn't recognize the wolf at her door, and you claimed she was so wise." He snarled. "I ripped open her belly and fed on her heart. I spared a cup of blood, just for you, my sweet! Kiss me, Little Red Hood, and I will

> This close the contents smelled like a butcher's shop, and her stomach roiled.

feast on your flesh."

He hauled Charlotte towards him. She screamed and struggled, but he howled in triumph. She grabbed the mug and smashed it against his face. He yelped, and let her go.

She sprinted for the door. Behind her the wolf cursed in pain. Charlotte was out of the cottage in a shot and running for the cover of the forest. She had played all her life there and knew the area well. She made a beeline for the river.

The front door banged open, and the man yelled, "Run fast, little Lottie, but you'll never escape me. I have your scent. I can track you over oceans and across fire." There was the sound of snapping and gnashing, but Charlotte didn't look back. She ducked under branches and jumped over tree roots in a panicked scramble to reach where Poppy was working.

She arrived at the stony riverbank, panting, and saw Poppy and the other laundresses on the other side. They were singing songs, chatting, and laughing. Poppy's skirts were tied up around her knees as she pounded a white sheet clean. The river between Charlotte and them was deep and swift.

"Help!" screamed Charlotte, and a terrible, hungering howl split the air. All the women's faces snapped up at that sound. They had heard it before. Poppy saw the fear etched deep on Charlotte's face.

In the blink of an eye Poppy twirled the heavy, damp

> The man ambled up to the river as if he was in no rush, but he sniffed the air and smiled.

sheet above her head, and muttered some words. It suddenly grew long and stiff as a board and she threw it over the water. The other laundresses held the sheet's edges to keep it steady. Charlotte dashed across it, skidding and splashing, and nearly falling into the river. Once Charlotte was across the sheet became limp again, and Poppy wound it in.

"He killed her!" she cried, when she fell into Poppy's arms. "He killed Granny. He's a wolf. He said he'll find me no matter where I go and kill me."

The women looked at each other. Several of their friends had gone missing. "Hide behind those baskets," Poppy ordered, and Charlotte did so.

At that moment the man ambled up to the river as if he was in no rush, but he sniffed the air and smiled. He kept his wolf face hidden. "Good afternoon ladies," he called out. "Is there a way across this river? I have a shirt that needs washing if you are willing."

Poppy cocked her hip and grinned at him. "If you're taking off that shirt I'm more than willing. I'll make you a bridge."

She picked up the sheet and spun it above her head, and it hardened like a board. She dropped it over the river.

After his first step on the board the man hesitated, and glanced down at the fast, babbling water. It appeared to unnerve him. He moved forwards cautiously, watching the water, not the other side.

Charlotte peeked at him from behind the baskets, frozen with fear.

When he was half-way across, Poppy called out, "Stop."

For the first time the man looked up, and he didn't like the expression on her face.

"I hear that wolves that walk around as men cannot change in running water. Let's find out." she tapped the sheet and it collapsed. The man fell into the water with a huge splash. Poppy made a winding motion and the heavy sheet twisted about his body, pinning his limbs. He thrashed and howled but it only entangled him more. The river's current caught him and dragged him downstream, slamming him against rocks, and pulling him under.

The last they saw of him was a flash of a blood-smeared sheet before he vanished under the churning water.

Charlotte stood up shakily, and Poppy hugged her. The entire group of women escorted her home to Nadine.

At her grandmother's funeral Charlotte wore her red cloak, and people whispered, "That's Little Red Hood. She met the wolf, and survived."

# The Cinder Wench

In a grand cemetery lined with evergreen trees, Grace wept as a casket containing her mother was lowered into its grave. Her father stood beside her, grim-faced with shock. Later, at the family home, Grace could not bear to be around anyone and wandered in the garden. She sat beside the pond that her mother loved and gazed at the ornamental fish swimming in the water. The biggest fish, a beautiful one with red and gold stripes, poked its nose out of the water: balanced on it was a hazelnut. A voice said, "Bury this in the garden and you will always have your mother's aid."

Grace picked a quiet spot to plant it. She cried over the little mound of earth for it reminded her of the burial earlier. Her tears fell on top of the soil and immediately the tree began to sprout.

Within the year the hazel tree was fully grown and bore many nuts. It was a popular tree with animals: squirrels bounded up its truck, seekihg nuts, and birds roosted there. Whenever Grace was scared or upset she liked to sit in the dappled shade of its leaves, listening to the wind stir the branches and the birds sing. She imagined it was her mother's voice giving her advice.

The following year Grace's father married an attractive widow named Amelia who had two pretty daughters Grace's age, named Trina and Jillian. Before the wedding Amelia had always treated Grace kindly, but as soon as she and her daughters moved into the house everything changed.

Amelia told her new husband that Grace was lazy and disrespectful, and resented the new women in the household. Trina and Jillian invented stories about how Grace burned holes in their gowns and stole their jewelry. Worst of all, Amelia related tales to her husband about Grace's mother, and even cast doubts over whether Grace was his child. She constantly pointed out how Grace's hair was auburn and his was fair, and how he was short and Grace was tall. Over time his attitude cooled toward his first daughter.

Within two months Amelia had control of the household. She gave Grace's room to Trina, and all of

Grace's clothes to Jillian. The scullery maid was let go and Grace forced to do her work, dress in rags, and sleep beside the hearth in the kitchen. One day Trina called Grace the Cinder Wench because Grace was often grey from the ashes of the fire. From that point on, the three women only used that name for Grace, or worse.

The other servants were replaced, and after six months no one knew that Grace had once been a noblewoman. Since the mistress of the house treated Grace so badly the other servants thought nothing of giving her extra chores, hitting her, or blaming her for any mishap. At night Grace often lay down on her hard bed by the fire hungry, tired, and bruised.

Whenever she found a few spare moments Grace sat under the hazel tree in the garden and prayed to her mother for help. All she heard in response was the cooing of the white doves that nested in its branches.

A year after Amelia and her daughters moved into the house, a royal page came to the door with a proclamation. The king's son, Prince Vincent, had come of age and was seeking a bride. His father was holding three balls, to which all the noblewomen in the kingdom, and beyond, were invited.

Amelia and her daughters exploded into a tizzy of excitement. For weeks all they discussed were their plans for their three dresses, how they would arrange their hair, and what they would say to charm the prince. Grace had an eye for style, and Amelia saved a lot of money by having Grace adjust dresses and fix their hair.

Inwardly, Grace despaired. She realized the more she did for the women the harder it would be for her to get away from them. One afternoon she tried to meet her father privately so she could ask for new clothes for the ball. Amelia intercepted her, and berated her for trying to interrupt her father while he was working. She drove Grace back to the kitchen where the cook had her scrub pots.

The day of the first ball arrived, and Grace was busy from dawn helping her stepmother and sisters prepare. She ironed gowns, adjusted ruffles, curled hair, laced corsets, polished jewels, and applied make-up. The three women were a dazzling sight by the evening.

"I bet you would love to go to the ball," Trina said to Grace in a cruel tone as they waited outside for the carriage to pull up to the front of the house.

Grace's father looked at his daughter, and his features softened. Amelia noticed instantly. "She would embarrass us in such prestigious company. She can't even keep her nails clean!"

Grace hid her hands behind her back, and her father looked away from her. The carriage pulled up, and he helped Trina and Jillian to climb inside. Amelia grabbed Grace by the arm, and hissed at her quietly. "Don't think I didn't see you butter up your father. There is a basin of lentils in the kitchen. Separate out the bad ones by the

time we come back or it will go badly for you."

Her father turned to help his wife into the carriage. Amelia smiled sweetly at Grace, and patted her on the cheek. "Enjoy your evening," she trilled.

Grace retired to the kitchen and discovered the massive basin of lentils. She slumped at the big table, wondering how she would complete the task. An odd tapping at the door caught her attention and she opened it. Two doves flew in and landed at the table.

One of them cocked her head at Grace. "Would you like us to help?" She sounded remarkably similar to Grace's mother.

Grace was temporarily silenced by surprise, but after she recovered, she replied "Yes please!"

She spread the lentils on the table and with amazing speed and accuracy the doves separated the good ones from pieces of grit and withered lentils.

Grace watched in astonishment, and laughed. Her spirits lifted. It felt like she had not smiled in a long time.

When the two piles were sorted, the other dove spoke. "Would you like to go to the ball?"

"Why, of course!"

"Wash up, and go to the hazel tree outside. Shake the trunk and open the nut that falls."

Grace did as she was bid, and when the nut fell from the tree she knocked it against a rock. It opened easily. Something glittered inside. She pulled at it and miraculously an entire silk gown emerged. It was indigo like the heavens and embroidered with stars. There were also two shoes of pearl and jewels fashioned like stars. Tears of gratitude welled in Grace's eyes.

The doves landed on a branch above Grace. "Do not tarry. Dress. We will summon your carriage."

The doves knocked against the hazel tree with their beaks. The trunk hinged open with a deep groan. A carriage made of copper, driven by four milk-white steeds, rushed out. A driver and a footman, clad in black livery, accompanied the carriage.

The footman hopped off and opened the door for Grace. She thanked him and climbed in. The doves fluttered by her window. "You must be back by midnight, for this spell will vanish by then."

She promised to remember, and waved farewell.

Grace's carriage was one of the last to pull up at the castle but it caused a stir among the guests. First, no one recognized the crest on its doors, and everyone was struck by the elegance and beauty of the woman who emerged.

Prince Vincent was outside, already exhausted from the small talk and the pressure from the array of women who were striving for his attention. His stood with his best friend Michael, who had been trying to ward off the most irritating ladies.

"I feel like a prize bull up for auction!" Vincent complained to Michael. "What was father thinking?"

> There were also two shoes of pearl and jewels fashioned like stars. Tears of gratitude welled in Grace's eyes.

# The Cinder Wench

They were taking a break in the shadows by the doorway, where they could watch those who entered to narrow down the field.

Michael shrugged, "What any royal father thinks: succession and children! He's fed up with waiting. Those two Trina and Jillian were pretty."

Vincent threw his hands in the air, "Just like the rest, fawning and fake. And their awful, pushy mother!"

"This is why your father is taking matters into his hands. You expect too much."

A wave of whispers reached the young men, and they noticed Grace sweep up the steps.

Michael nudged Vincent. "What a beauty!" But his friend made no reply, for he looked like he'd been hit by a thunderbolt.

"Is it too much to hope that she is also intelligent?" Vincent set off after her, eager to find out.

Men had already flocked to Grace when Vincent caught up with her, but they stepped aside for him. He claimed her first dance, and her second, and her third— he did not leave her side all evening.

As it approached midnight, Grace remembered the warning of the doves, and sent Vincent off to find her a refreshment. As she descended the steps the carriage pulled up and the footman helped her in. Prince Vincent appeared at the top of the steps, and called out, but the driver cracked his whip and the carriage pulled away instantly.

Grace was back at her family home before midnight, and on the twelfth stroke the carriage vanished. She hid the beautiful clothing in the nut, put on her ash dress, and rubbed cinders on her body and hair. When her family returned all they could speak of was the mysterious lady the prince danced with throughout the night. Grace helped the women undress, and tried not to smile at their speculations about the woman's identity.

The next morning Grace was up early to help Amelia, Trina, and Jillian dress for the second ball. At one point,

Amelia noticed Grace smiling and humming as she pinned flowers in Trina's hair.

"What are you so pleased about?" Amelia snapped.

"Helping you look beautiful for the ball makes me happy," she replied. The three women regarded Grace with hard, suspicious stares.

Amelia gave Grace a push. "You're finished here. There's a big sack of seeds down in the kitchen. Separate all the good ones from the bad by the time we return."

From the kitchen Grace heard the carriage collect the group to bring them to the ball. She found the large sack of seeds just as the doves appeared and offered their aid again. Within a short time the seeds were sorted into two piles. "Shake the hazel tree," they told her, "and discover what you'll receive tonight."

With gladness in her heart Grace did as she was bid, and when she opened the nut she discovered a dress of green silk embroidered with flowers, silver shoes, and a necklace with gleaming gems. The doves summoned the carriage, and this time it was made of silver and driven by black horses.

At the castle, Prince Vincent waited anxiously for her arrival. Many of the guests noticed his distracted air, and reproached the King because the prince was not giving equal attention to their daughters. The King listened and nodded sympathetically, but secretly he was encouraged by his son's devotion to the young woman.

> He claimed her first dance, and her second, and her third... he did not leave her side all evening.

As soon as Grace appeared in the ballroom, Prince Vincent asked her to dance, and he didn't glance at another woman for the rest of the night.

During their time together the couple laughed and talked, although Grace evaded all questions about her background, and even refused to give her name to the Prince. "Tonight, let us just be a man and a woman, without titles or expectations, who enjoy being together," she said.

As midnight approached Grace tried to distract Vincent so she could leave, but he was determined to stay with her for as long as possible.

She managed to slip away when it was close to midnight, but Vincent was prepared. His friend Michael had been waiting in a carriage, and when Grace's vehicle shot off Michael followed. Grace noticed the pursuit, and called out to the driver to go faster.

He cracked his whip and the horses doubled their speed. A thick mist descended after their carriage and obscured their path. Within minutes Michael had to abandon the chase. Vincent was disappointed, but determined that he wouldn't lose his lady the subsequent night.

Grace was stepping out of the carriage when it disappeared. She hurried to hide her outfit, and returned to being the Cinder Wench.

Later that night, Amelia and her daughters returned in a foul humor. It was obvious to everyone that the prince was only interested in one woman. As they undressed they complained bitterly about their competitor and offered many unsavory suggestions about her background and her intentions for the prince. Grace kept her expression neutral despite her desire to laugh at their guesswork.

A few hours later, Grace faced another long day of preparations with Amelia and her daughters. She listened to them scheme to get the Prince's attention and even sabotage the mysterious lady. Amelia noticed Grace's good spirits, and sent her to the kitchen to sort through a bucket of peas when they were leaving for the castle.

Once again the doves arrived and sifted the peas, and Grace ran out to the garden to discover her final outfit. That night it was a dress of gold silk, with gold slippers and a gold tiara. The carriage was painted gold, and it was drawn by four horses, shimmering like the sun.

Her arrival at the ball caused a commotion, for no one could compete with Grace's beauty or style. The prince appeared instantly at Grace's side, and never left her throughout the night. At one point Trina faked a fainting spell in front of the prince while Jillian attempted to spill wine over Grace, but Grace was aware of the plan and sidestepped Jillian. Instead, the red wine ended up over Trina's face and gown. The two girls began screaming at each other until Amelia pulled them away, rebuking

them for causing a spectacle.

That night, Grace became lost in the joy of the evening: the lively music, the dancing, the food, and her handsome, attentive partner. She wasn't sure what would happen in the future, so she savored every moment with the Prince. Suddenly, Grace was aware that it was almost midnight. She managed to elude Vincent, but earlier Michael had spread tar on the steps to slow her down. She struggled to reach the waiting carriage, aware of time ticking away. Vincent stood at the top of the stairs and called down to her.

One of Grace's shoes got stuck in the sticky tar, and Grace had to leap into the carriage. The carriage drove away swiftly, but it only carried her a short distance before it disappeared. Grace had to walk the rest of the way home with only one shoe. She returned mere minutes before her stepmother and sisters, but they were so angry about the night's events they didn't notice that Grace's face and hands were clean.

After the frenetic preparations for the balls, the pace of life slowed at the house, except that Amelia and her daughters took their frustrations out on Grace. They had her running up and down the stairs on errands, usually accompanied by a cruel taunt and an occasional slap.

Grace treasured her memories of the three merry evenings, and especially how Vincent held her in his arms as they danced. Amelia boxed her ears once for day dreaming, but Grace didn't shed a tear. She was

> The prince was looking for his lady, and he had in his possession her slipper. Whosoever fit the shoe would be his wife.

determined never to cry in front of the three women again. In fact, she began to lay plans to escape and make her own way in the world. After her taste of freedom and happiness she was no longer willing to accept humiliation and servitude. Amelia noticed Grace's change in demeanor and tripled her workload.

A week later, the royal page came to the door with another proclamation: the prince was looking for his lady, and he had in his possession her slipper. Whosoever fit the shoe would be his wife.

The prince was traveling from house to house, and Trina and Jillian waited for their turn in a fever of excitement. Rumors abounded that the shoe was exceptionally small and designed for a dainty foot, but the two girls had tiny feet and were positive it would fit one of them.

Finally, the day arrived and the prince visited their home. Grace watched him arrive from the kitchen window, and her heart beat faster. Amelia and their daughters hatched a plan out of earshot of Grace. When the prince showed Trina the shoe, she asked to go into another room to try it on for modesty's sake.

The prince consented, and Amelia accompanied her daughter to the next room. Despite all her efforts, Trina could not shove her heel into the shoe. Amelia picked up a knife. "I will cut off a piece of your heel," she said. "The pain will pass quickly when you are crowned queen."

Trina paled, but nodded assent. She clamped her hands over her mouth, and muffled her scream as her mother carved off a section of her heel. Blood poured out, and they tried to stem its flow. Trina put on the shoe and walked weakly into the room where the prince waited.

He was surprised, for he knew that Trina was not the woman he loved, but he had given his word, and the shoe fit her. Vincent steeled his heart, and prepared to take the respectable course of action.

At that moment two doves tapped at the window and cried out:

> The shoe fits
> But it's been forced,
> Her heel is cut,
> Observe its bloody
> course.

The prince leaned closer and saw a smear of blood on the shoe. "Please remove your foot," he ordered.

Trina tried to protest but the prince insisted. When he saw the chunk of missing flesh he was sickened, but also pleased she had failed.

"Let your other daughter try it on," he commanded.

This time Amelia persuaded the prince that she needed to clean the shoe of blood, and she took it into the next room with Jillian.

Jillian could get her heel in, but not her toes. Amelia held up the knife.

"I will cut off your two smallest toes," she said. "The pain will pass quickly when you are crowned queen."

Jillian nearly passed out from the pain as her mother

sawed through her toes, but afterwards her mutilated foot fit the shoe.

The prince's face darkened when he saw Jillian walk stiffly into the room. This time he expected mischief, even as the doves fluttered at the window and called out their warning.

"My lady, show me your foot," he said. Amelia and Jillian protested, and called upon the prince to be honorable and adhere to his promise. Instead the Prince warned Jillian that treason was punishable by hanging.

Jillian took off the shoe, and revealed her maimed foot.

The prince reined in his exasperation, "Do you have any other daughters?" He asked Amelia.

She smiled, and answered no.

At that the doves caused a racket at the window.

*"She has no other daughter, true,*
*But another girl resides here too."*

The Prince stood and ordered Amelia to bring the woman in front of him immediately.

Despite the grime and the rags the prince instantly recognized Grace. He led her to a chair and bade her to sit down. He knelt before her and slipped on the shoe. They stood up, hugged, and kissed for the first time while Amelia and her daughters stood aghast.

Then Grace took the three nuts from her pocket and showed Vincent the marvel of her gowns and dresses. She produced the other golden slipper and put it on.

For their deceit the prince stripped all titles and privileges from Amelia and her daughters. They were given jobs in the castle's kitchens. Grace pleaded for leniency for her father, but the prince could not forgive his cruel treatment of his daughter. "You have a kind heart, my love, but he will serve in the kitchens beside his wife, for as long as you were made to serve them," he ordered.

On the day Vincent and Grace were married, two white doves flew into the church, and dropped the wedding bands onto the couple's outstretched palms.

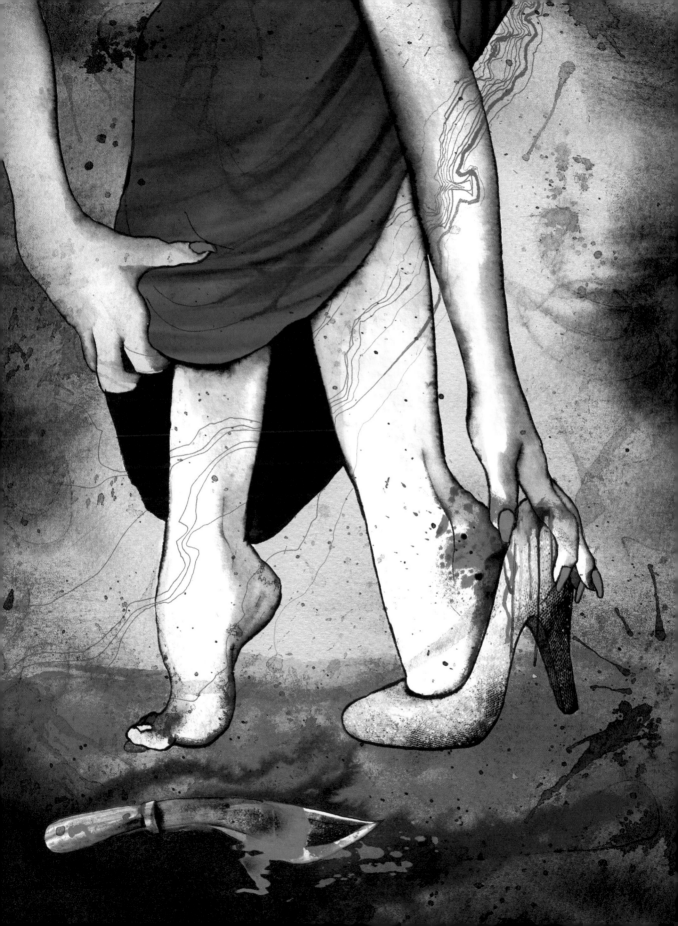

# Beauty and the Beast

Many years ago a wealthy merchant lived in a busy port town trading spices and textiles with the East. He had three sons and three daughters, the youngest of whom was his pride and joy. She was so kind and attractive that everyone called her Beauty – apart from her two sisters Catherine and Elizabeth, who referred to her as "the bookworm".

Cat and Beth (as they were called at home) enjoyed parties and dressing up, and could not understand why their sister preferred the library and the company of books. They decided Beauty thought she was better than them, so they picked on her at every opportunity. Their brothers were enamoured of hunting and gambling, and rarely saw their sisters, except at Sunday breakfast or an evening soirée.

Yet, disaster occurred: due to a series of reckless investments, and the loss of his trading ships in a storm, the merchant was bankrupted overnight. His colleagues expressed sorrow at his misfortune, but refused to help him. The banks seized his assets. The lone possession remaining was his deceased wife's family home in the country. His children were stunned. They were used to having everything they desired. Going without or working was foreign to them.

Cat and Beth were each positive at least one of their suitors would marry them. The news of their father's diminished circumstances spread like wildfire however, and the girls discovered their beaus were too busy to meet them. Invitations to parties dried up and the family's former friends no longer greeted them in the street.

The oldest son joined the army, while another took an apprenticeship with a silversmith. The rest packed up their few belongings and left the city for the rustic house in the country. Luckily for Beauty, no one wanted the books, and she was able to bring many of them with her. The youngest son Daniel took a liking to farming, and Beauty began to learn how to run a household. Their father's health took a turn for the worse from the stress, and he spent most of his days in his study, sifting through the copious paperwork.

# Beauty and the Beast

Cat and Beth hated the countryside. They made fun of the manners and fashion of their neighbours and were subsequently unpopular. The change was a shock to Beauty, too, but she decided to make the best of it. Soon the local people took a shine to Beauty, and after a while she was never short of help if she needed it. Several men offered marriage, but Beauty refused them all, saying she wished to care for her father. This infuriated Cat and Beth even more. They took to treating Beauty like a servant. If they ever saw her taking a few moments to read a book they berated her laziness. They, on the other hand, were always too frail to do chores. Beauty, conscious of her father's ill-health and aware of her sisters' frustrations, refused to argue with them.

On a rare occasion she would climb a nearby hill to watch the clouds sail by and wish she could fling a hook in them and fly away from her troubles.

Six months later her father received word that one of his ships had returned to port. He set off to discover if he could recover any money. Cat and Beth were delirious with excitement, and pestered him with requests for clothes and jewelry. When he asked Beauty what she would like, she asked for a rose. Cat and Beth sneered at her decision.

The merchant's trip was unsuccessful. The ship's goods were taken by his creditors to cover his debts. After a week away, he returned home on his horse with a few baubles to keep his daughters happy. Due to his distress and distraction, he got caught in a squall and turned about. He found himself in a strange part of the countryside, blinded by the dark, sodden, and hungry.

A flash of lightning illuminated an ornate set of gates, overgrown with ivy. He managed to push them open and squeeze through with his horse. The stables were dry and clean, so he left his steed and went to the main house to beg for shelter.

The door to the mansion opened at his knock, and he marveled at its grand size, elegant decoration, and expensive furnishings. He could find no one home, but there were candles burning in the dining room. The table was set for one, with a generous meal of pheasant, vegetables, and wine. He waited for someone to appear, and in the end, with spoken thanks, he ate the meal. Afterwards, he found a bedroom with a cheerful fire, and he rested for the night.

In the morning a new suit of clothing awaited him. The sun shone, and his spirits soared. He wondered who his invisible benefactor could be as he walked through the graceful gardens to the stables. One section was dedicated to roses, and as the merchant passed them and smelled their perfume, he remembered his promise to Beauty.

He picked one large rose the color of a spring dawn, and at once heard a fierce growling and snorting. A person dressed in gentleman's clothing but with a huge boar's head and jutting tusks, a scorpion's tail, and talons on his fingers came rushing toward him.

The merchant screamed in shock, which enraged the creature. He towered over the merchant, his eyes blazing and his claws spread, as if he were about to wring the old man's neck.

"Mercy!" cried the merchant, cowering.

"Thief! I gave you shelter and food and you repay me by stealing my favorite rose. Make peace with your maker for you will die today."

"My lord-"

"Don't flatter me! Call me Beast, for that's what I am, and beasts do not spare those who trespass against them."

"It was for my youngest daughter, please spare me Master Beast, for I can't make my peace unless I look upon her sweet face again."

The Beast reined in his temper with a visible effort. "You have a daughter?"

"Three of them, kind sir."

"And do they love you?"

The merchant considered this, and discovered he wondered about Cat and Beth's true feelings, but was certain of Beauty's devotion. Tremendous love welled up in his heart for all his children and he could only nod assent, for his voice was stolen by emotion.

"Then you may go home to say farewell. If one of them returns in your place I will spare you." The beast thrust his face close to the merchant, so his tusks poked the old man's face under the eyes. "Do *not* try to cheat me. If you,

or a daughter, does not return, I will hunt you down, gut you in front of your family, and slaughter them after."

Trembling, the merchant nodded,

The Beast handed the rose to the merchant. "I hope it was worth it."

He escorted the merchant to the stable, and placed a beautiful bridle upon his horse. "When it is time to come back, whisper to the horse, 'Take me to the Beast's palace,' and it will know the way."

The merchant was in a state of shock for most of his journey home, unsure of what to say to his family. When he approached the house, Beauty was the first to see him, and she ran out, smiling.

He handed her the rose. When he witnessed the love and joy in her face he wept. Later, with his son and daughters around him, he related his tale. Daniel was determined to call upon his brothers to hunt the Beast, and Cat and Beth blamed Beauty for the situation.

"I will take your place, father," Beauty said. At that he wept again, for he could not imagine a better daughter. He sat up straight. "It was my lapse. I will spend the next week with you before I face my fate."

Beauty noticed the greyness in her father's cheeks, and the tremble in his hands. She knew he could not withstand any more shocks.

The following morning, Beauty rose early, left her father a note, and put the Beast's bridle upon the horse. "Take me to the Beast's palace," she said.

> "Call me Beast, for that's what I am, and beasts do not spare those who trespass against them."

# Beauty and the Beast

Several hours later she arrived at the overgrown gates of the Beast's estate. But inside, all was in good order. Beauty combed down her horse and entered the mansion. She was scared, but determined to be brave. She explored the rooms, but spent most of her time in the library. There were tall windows along one side, to allow for plenty of light and splendid views, but otherwise it was lined from ceiling to floor with books.

Before she knew it, evening arrived. When she walked into the large reception room, four statues of women with lit torches in their hands stepped down from their plinths. A gasp of fear escaped Beauty. The faces of the statues turned to regard her with their blind eyes. They gestured for her to follow them. The eerie procession led her into a huge dining room with a table long enough to seat thirty guests. The room was lit with candelabras, and a fire burned in a stone fireplace carved with lions. Each of the statues took up a spot in the corner of the room. At one end of the table there were two places set for dinner, with gold plates and crystal goblets.

Beauty sat down, and waited. A few minutes later the door opened and the Beast entered the room. Beauty's eyes opened wide and she barely restrained a cry. Her father had described him well, but nothing prepared her for the creature. He wore a doublet of black velvet with lace ruffles, and silk breeches. She noticed he did not wear shoes for his feet were like wolf's paws. He approached

carefully, as if allowing her time to get used to him.

She stood out of courtesy to greet him even though her legs shook. She wondered if he would kill her tonight or tomorrow.

"Good evening, Lord Beast," she said, and she was amazed her voice remained steady. "My name is Beauty, and I have come in my father's place. It is my fault he picked the rose. I never imagined my simple request might cost him his life."

The Beast drew near, and his snout wrinkled as he inhaled a deep breath, but Beauty noticed his eyes were kind. His tail whisked about.

"You came willingly?"

"Yes."

The Beast indicated she should sit, and she did.

"You are a brave woman," he said in a deep voice, and picked up a carving knife. Beauty watched his every move, expecting him to plunge it into her heart. Instead he began to cut thin slices of pheasant with expert skill.

"You are my guest, Beauty," he said, as he served her food. "You will want for nothing. Your apartment has been prepared, with a wardrobe of gowns and a safe full of jewels. You have free movement in the house and gardens. I ask that you dine with me each evening, but I will not force my presence upon you otherwise." His voice changed and dripped with disgust. "I know how odious I am to look upon."

"But I may not leave?"

His raised his voice, "If you do your life and your

father's life is forfeit!"

Beauty flinched. The Beast stood. "That was rude of me. I apologize. My nature..." he snorted, "I am... was a gentleman. I mean you no harm Beauty. I would rather die than hurt you, but you must stay here with me." He clenched and unclenched his clawed fists, and looked down at them. A strangled sound escaped him. "I will leave for the night." He bowed, and loped out of the room.

Beauty ate little, and when she was finished the four statues sedately led her to a suite set aside for her. As Beast promised there were dresses and jewels, but as Beauty walked through the exquisite rooms she was most aware of their emptiness and silence.

The next day breakfast was waiting for her in a sunny parlor with a view of the rose garden. She came to love this room the best for it was small and intimate, and she was less conscious of her solitude.

Beauty had become used to running a household and taking care of her family, so the absence of anything to do was a shock. All her meals were prepared for her, and if she asked out loud for anything it had the uncanny knack of appearing some time later. At first she enjoyed these luxuries, but quite soon she knew the entire palace from the smallest garret to the bottom cellar, so there was nothing new to discover. She had no company during the day. The statues only came to life if they had something to show her. Beauty spent much of her time in the library reading. She attempted to find any histories of the estate or the Beast's family, but there were gaps in the bookshelves that indicated they had been removed, just as there were gaps on the walls where certain portraits used to hang.

Beauty came to look forward to meeting the Beast for their evening meals. Over time they spent more time together, playing cards or chess, and discussing literature and philosophy.

"I never used to read," Beast said when Beauty praised his knowledge of books. They were sitting by the stone fireplace, drinking a glass of brandy each. "I only thought of pleasure, hunting, and being in the company of others."

"What happened?"

Beast stared at the fire, brooding. "I became frightful."

Beauty placed her hand on his arm. "You have a good heart, Beast."

At her touch Beast clamped his rough hand over hers. "Then marry me, Beauty!"

Beauty recoiled, and seeing her surprise the Beast began to speak quickly: "You must know I love you, Beauty, and I can give you anything you desire: money, gowns—"

Beauty yanked her hand away and stood up, arms crossed. "I had all of that! It's empty, just like this house. Pretty, but a prison all the same. When I lost everything all that sustained me was my family... and their love," she turned away so he would not see the tears in her eyes.

"You miss them," he said, his voice hollow. She nodded. "Then come with me." He picked up a candlestick and led her to a study that had a small nondescript mirror hanging on its wall. He held up the light. "This will show you those you care about most."

At first Beauty only perceived her and Beast's face, but she concentrated on those she loved. First she saw Daniel, with an arm around Martha, the town's baker. Clearly, they were courting. The mirror's surface misted, and cleared to show her two sisters in each other's company as usual, conversing and embroidering rather poorly. Finally she saw the dear face of her father, a shawl over his shoulders, sitting in his study, staring out the window. He had the appearance of one grief-stricken.

The mirror went dark again. Beauty was so delighted that she hugged Beast. "Thank you," she whispered, and kissed his cheek.

Beast let her go reluctantly. "You can only use it once a day, but you may come in here as you wish."

Initially Beauty found the long, quiet days more bearable once she could spy upon her family. She tried to wait until midday, but sometimes she consulted it as soon as she was dressed in the morning. She witnessed her brother making wedding preparations, and her sisters planning new outfits for the occasion, but her father rarely seemed to do much other than sit and languish.

One time, as her father's face faded, the thought flashed through her mind, *I wonder what Beast is doing now?* Immediately the mirror showed her an image of Beast. He was in forest nearby, hiding in undergrowth. He wasn't wearing any clothes, and what she could see of his body was entirely covered in thick hair. He crouched on all fours, very still. There was a flash of movement, and Beast bounded out, feral and quick. His scorpion tail sliced through the air and hit a deer in the neck. He followed through by slashing it with his front hand. Blood spurted, and the animal fell to the earth, its legs kicking.

A small gasp escaped Beauty's lips, "Oh Beast!"

At that Beast turned and looked directly at Beauty just as the image faded away.

That night they ate venison together. Beast was quieter than usual, and picked at his food. Beauty tried to fill the silences by talking about her family and the forthcoming wedding. When they sat by the fire later, he leaned forward and took her hand gently.

"Dearest Beauty, will you be my wife?"

Beauty's cheeks flamed, and she looked at his eyes, so human in his beast face. "Beast, you have been kind to me and I esteem you greatly..."

Beast let go of her hand. "I sense a but," he said.

"You are my jailer. You cannot expect a prisoner to wed the warden."

He nodded, and released a heavy sigh. "I will set you free."

He reached into his pocket and took out a ring. "Twist the ring three times and think of the place you want to be. I ask that you use the ring to return after seven days... but, only if you so desire."

With that he gave her a large bag of gold coins to help take care of her family and pay for the wedding. She put on her best dress and packed a trunk. The Beast stood in front of her, forlorn. Beauty hugged Beast, and whispered, "I will come back."

She put on the ring and twisted it three times. In an instant she was in her bedroom in the farmhouse. She ran down the stairs and found her father in the study. He was so surprised and overjoyed he lost his breath for a short time, but he recovered as he embraced her. Daniel, Cat, and Beth crowded into the room and they had a noisy reunion. The girls were astonished by her pretty dress,

> He wasn't wearing any clothes, and what she could see of his body was entirely covered in thick hair.

and how well she looked. Beauty gave each of them beautiful gifts.

Later, when it was only her and her father sharing tea in the kitchen, she handed him the bag of coins.

He wept, and tried to refuse it. "I should have spent your childhood taking care of my real treasure, my children."

She gripped his hand. "You did what you thought was best. Now, use this wisely."

Beauty spent the next few days helping with wedding preparations, and meeting her brother's future in-laws. On the sixth day the wedding took place. There was a party afterwards in the garden of the family home. Tables groaned under the weight of the food and there were barrels of beer and bottles of wine. Musicians played all day, and everyone danced.

Beauty was radiant, although she had taken some pains not to outshine the bride. All the single men vied to dance with her. Many of them complimented her but didn't seem particularly interested in what she had to say, and expected her to listen to them brag about their achievements. Cat and Beth danced a couple of times but mostly they sat and gossiped.

The more Beauty danced the more weary she became of the dull conversations. She found herself wondering what the Beast was doing, and thinking of little anecdotes to tell him upon her return. She realized she was smiling at that thought, and with a jolt recognized she was looking forward to seeing him again.

At that moment her dance partner whirled her off under the shade of a tree and drew her roughly to him.

"Stop!" she whispered, trying not to cause a scene and disrupt the celebrations.

The man laughed, and tried to kiss her. Beauty struggled to get out of his grip. "Don't act the lady!" he leered, and he had beast eyes in a human face. "We all know you're a rich man's mistress."

Anger at his assumption boiled up in her, and Beauty pushed him off. "And we all know you are a drunken buffoon!"

He attempted to grab her again, and this time she evaded him neatly.

She retired to her room for the night.

The following day Beauty made ready to return to Beast. Everyone pleaded with her to stay, even for an extra day. Beauty was most surprised at the red eyes and tears from her sisters. What she didn't realize was they had used onions to generate the effect. They hoped that if their sister overstayed that the Beast might devour her when she returned.

Most difficult for Beauty to resist were the entreaties of her father. They wore her down until she agreed to stay an extra day. That night she had a terrible dream in which Beast howled in pain in the forest, and she chased after him. When she finally reached him his fur was matted in blood. He held out his clawed hands: "You forgot your Beast."

When Beauty woke it was not yet dawn. Her heart raced and she was filled with a terrible dread. She dressed quickly, left a note for her family, and twisted the ring to return to the Beast's palace.

She searched everywhere but could find no sign of him. A large meal was set for two in the dining room, but nothing had been touched. A single rose lay on the table.

She found the statues and begged that they tell her where Beast was, but they remained mute and unmoving. Finally, she went into the room in the study. The mirror was smashed on the floor.

She picked up a sliver of looking glass, and pictured Beast. She glimpsed a faint image of him, lying in the rose garden.

Beauty bolted out of the room and ran to the garden. Beast lay still on the grass, rose petals scattered around him.

Beauty fell beside him and cupped her hands around his beast face. "Beast, wake up!" she cried. He did not respond. "I am here, as I promised."

Beast's eyes opened, but his voice was faint. "I saw you dancing with those men. They were so handsome and normal. I realized someone like you could never love someone like me. I am wretched."

Beauty leaned down and kissed him. "Darling Beast," she said, "You are more handsome than any of the men I danced with." She hugged him, and in that moment understood the depth of her feelings for him.

"I love you. Will you marry me, Beast?"

He cried out, and she let him go, afraid she had hurt him.

Instead, he was shaking from a transformation. The tusks melted, the tail disappeared, the fur shed, and his face became that of a handsome young man.

Beauty helped him to his feet, unsure. She had become so used to Beast. This man was a stranger to her.

"Darling Beauty, you have freed me from a curse put upon me by a powerful magician I slighted. My name is Griffen." At this he bowed, and kissed her hand.

When he looked up at her she saw his familiar eyes, and her heart recognized him.

"I was unable to explain my situation or how to break the spell, for that would negate any cure." His smile was pure joy.

"But, I had long ago decided that I could live as a beast if you remained in my life. Letting you go, knowing you may choose never to return, was agony."

Beauty reached out and touched his face. "Beast or man, you are the one for me."

> The tusks melted, the tail disappeared, the fur shed, and his face became that of a handsome young man.

# May and the Elf Knight

May was so named because she was born on the first, fresh day of that month, when the fragrant blossoms had not yet faded and summer stretched ahead in glorious potential.

Her father was a clever merchant who married her high-born mother for love and the privileges it would bestow upon his dynasty. May, and her two younger brothers — Jacques and Leon — knew only the best in life: education, good food, and a secure, happy home. Somehow, despite the advantages that May's fair features gave her over her rougher, plainer brothers, she remained unspoiled. If anything, she was too trusting, too easily persuaded—a trait that worried her parents in their private moments together.

May's brothers sometimes took advantage of her kind nature to play tricks on her, but she loved them fiercely and never told on them when their pranks brought trouble upon them all. In return, they taught her to wrestle, throw a punch, how to handle a knife, and where best to puncture a man if he became too familiar.

When May turned sixteen her parents held a feast in her honor. May understood that it was a prelude to the forthcoming jostling to win her hand in marriage. Her father was wealthy, her mother influential, and her pretty face was a bonus. Yet she did not wish to be a prize for an ambitious merchant or a lord down on his luck. Her romantic heart dreamed of a suitor who would cherish her for love, not advantage.

After the grand banquet May danced with the fawning men, and tried to stifle her laughs when Jacques and Leon made faces behind the backs of her partners. In between dances she shared a goblet of wine with her brothers by an open window, glad of the breeze to cool her hot face.

"How do you put up with them?" Jacques asked. "Yorick has two left feet and Adam is a bore." Leon nodded in agreement with his brother; he was not very talkative because he was overly conscious of his stutter. "Thomas is sly and Gerard's a braggart. Stay away from the lot of them!"

May was about to murmur politely, "Oh, they're not so

bad," when she noticed a man standing in the corner of the room, near the table of refreshments. His eyes glinted in the candlelight in a bewitching fashion. He was the most beautiful man May had ever seen. Feeling an instant, intense attraction for him, her breath seized.

The chatter of her brothers faded away, and the room became hazy. Only the tall, distinguished gentleman was clear to her. She was about to walk over to him boldly but then hesitated, knowing, from his direct gaze, that they would meet outside in the garden that night. May nodded, and his perfect lips curled up in a satisfied smile. Seeing his pleasure, she thought her heart might burst with joy.

"Are you away with the fairies, May?" Jacques's voice suddenly registered with her.

"It's the heat and the wine," she replied, "I'm awfully drowsy. I think I'll make my excuses and retire."

Jacques laughed. "Most people use these festivities as an excuse not to go to bed!" Just then, the musicians broke into a lively tune, and many of the revelers picked partners and began to dance.

May slipped away, grateful to leave the noise and the crowds. The tall, handsome stranger was the only thing on her mind. When she returned to her room, she packed a bag, filling it with all the jewelry she'd been given as gifts that night. They would need money to start their life together, she realized. May remembered the bag of coins that her parents kept in their bedroom. She sneaked in

and took it.

A nagging thought about the strangeness of this sudden passion lingered in her mind. But the idea of not meeting him brought on feelings of anxiety and panic that were only soothed when she focused instead on their future together. Then, happiness consumed her.

Later, while everyone in the house slumbered — more deeply than usual because of their excesses that night — May put on her best dress and a cloak, slung her satchel of supplies over her shoulder, and moved quietly through the household. Not even the dogs raised their heads when she passed.

"My love," she whispered when she found the man in the garden standing beside the willow tree, the moonlight illuminating his sublime face. "I am here as you commanded."

The stranger smiled his perfect smile and said, "Oh, how easily they run to please me." He laughed. May didn't understand the joke, but she laughed with him. "Have you brought everything — money, jewels?" he asked.

"Oh yes. My parents won't mind once we are married."

He chuckled again, and touched an elaborate silver brooch that fastened his cloak about his neck. "Then let us not tarry. Your father has a valuable mare, I understand? You should saddle her and meet me on the road outside the house, and we will ride away together."

May trembled as she put the harness on the horse, desperate to be with her knight as soon as possible. She

The pain of his words was as horrible as the thought of chiding him for his cruelty.

joined him on the road, and they urged their horses into a quick trot away from her parents' stately home, and away from her town. May was thrilled at the prospect of adventure.

After a few miles they slowed down as they entered the outskirts of a forest. Only narrow beams of moonlight pierced the leaf canopy of the ancient trees, and the knight used this as an excuse to take the reins from May's hands and lead them both. His sight was extraordinarily sharp, he told her.

The knight noticed her furtive, nervous glances. "We will not be attacked," he reassured her. "We are in my territory now." He inhaled deeply and beamed. "I'd like to see your father or your brothers last one night in this domain. Especially the youngest – that idiot who stutters?"

The pain of his words was as horrible as the thought of chiding him for his cruelty. Both misery and love resided in May's heart.

Suddenly a chill breeze picked up, whooshing through the branches and the undergrowth. Wild beasts cried out, and strange birds emitted piercing calls. It seemed like words were hidden in the wind whipping past her ears, and they warned her of the elf knight.

His love is forged from charm and lies,
All who listen wilt and die.

"Soon we will be at the heart of my land and you shall have your reward," the man announced, adjusting his cloak and pressing his fingers against the brooch.

"What will happen then, my lord?" May asked.

"Why, I will do what I did to the other seven ladies who betrayed their families. I will chop off your head and throw your body in the river." He touched the brooch again.

A simpering smile stole unwillingly over May's face. Appalled, she could make no move against him.

"You're the same as the others," he added. "Easily bidden and easily dispatched."

Terrified, May's paralyzed fingers could barely fasten onto her horse's mane. No one knew she was gone yet. Who would rescue her?

The knight beheaded seven lovely maids, too pinned down by despair to save their own lives.

After a long, fearful journey, May and the knight came to a clearing by a bend in a wide, rapidly flowing river. The water roared, a hungry sound. He lifted her from her mount. In that moment, certain she was about to perish, May was struck by the unearthly beauty of the place: the icy moonlight, the silver trees, and foaming river. It stirred within her a desperate desire to live – to explore and embrace the world. A new determination grew: she would not meet death meekly.

The knight drew his sword. "Kneel, and accept justice for your foolish heart!" he commanded.

"My lord, my gown is worth a great deal," pleaded May.

"It will be ruined if you lop my head off first."

"You are mistaken if you think you can beguile me with your flesh, since I care not for your kind. Quick now, disrobe! The river wants another ghost for company."

Shaking, May began to undress. "Please, my lord, avert your gaze." She feigned a high-pitched voice that made her sound weak and submissive.

The knight shook his head in wonder. "Rest assured, your modesty is unnecessary. Still, one final request." He turned his back.

May made a show of rustling her clothes so he thought her compliant. Then she crept up behind him, threw her dress over his head, and tore the brooch from his cloak. She stabbed the long pin into his neck as he thrashed around in pain. A geyser of blood erupted from the wound and sprayed over her face.

He slumped to his knees and collapsed with a gurgle.

For a long time, May stood, shuddering, above the knight's body. Then she put on her blood-soaked clothes and rolled his body into the river. It disappeared with a splash. She fancied the river rippled in satisfaction.

May held the brooch in her hand and considered the many ways she could use its power. She thought of the bones of the seven murdered women resting in the mud of the river bed, and their families who would never know what became of them. With all her might she threw the brooch into the river, hoping its power would appease the dead.

She quickly returned home and cleaned up before the household stirred. The extra horse in the stable was a puzzle, but everyone assumed that a guest would claim it eventually. No one ever did, though, and it became May's favorite mount.

Her family often commented that after her sixteenth birthday May matured and developed a healthy poise. As the years wore on she traveled on behalf of her father, and eventually took over his business. May had many suitors, but none of them ever inspired the same consuming passion she experienced for the dreaded Elf Knight.

On some moonlit nights May dreams of his cruel eyes, the forest river, and the ghosts of the slaughtered maidens.

She is always glad to wake up.

# Sleeping Beauty

It was *the* event of the year: the christening of Princess Talia, the longed-for first child of King Augustus and Queen Caroline. After the elaborate church ceremony, during which two women fainted from standing for too long in hot, heavy dresses, the gathering decamped to the castle for a lavish banquet.

Seated at a special table of honor were seven fairies, invited to bless Talia on her special day. The oldest, Cecily, wore a dress made of oak bark and leaves, and her hair rippled like a weeping willow. The youngest, Gillyfloss, smoothed out her dress of silk and rose petals, and tapped the fireflies that lit the crown of meadow flowers on her head. "Don't get dozy, you lot," Gillyfloss warned. It was her first Princess blessing and Gillyfloss wanted it to be perfect.

After the meal, the King and Queen called on the fairies to grant their beloved daughter a blessing. Gillyfloss would be the last to bestow a favor upon the Princess. "*Cecily will choose a crowd-pleaser*," Gillyfloss guessed.

Cecily floated to the cradle in which the princess cooed, and declared: "She shall be as beautiful as a summer morn, and loved by those who gaze upon her true." The hall burst into applause. Cecily returned to the table, and raised an eyebrow that challenged: "*Beat that!*"

As the fairies tried to out-do each other, Gillyfloss became increasingly vexed. She realized she would have to wish intelligence or wisdom for Talia, because the other fairies were giving her a "voice sweeter than a nightingale" or "the grace of a fawn". *She will be Queen one day. Beauty fades and she can't sing and dance in a council meeting.*

Just as Gillyfloss was about to present her gift, a terrible commotion broke out at the back of the hall, followed by a flash and the smell of singed flesh. All the fairies leaped up for they sensed the arrival of Millicent, an ancient fairy who had not been seen in decades. She was also Fairy Godmother to King Augustus.

She appeared from a puff of violet smoke. Cecily snorted at the theatrics. Millicent flashed her a look of such fury that the leaves on Cecily's dress withered instantly.

"Why was I not invited, Godson?" she thundered, and she fixed Queen Caroline with a suspicious glare. The queen

was reputed to dislike her husband's family tradition of associating with fairies.

The king stood and said, "My dearest Godmother, my sincere apologies. I sent several couriers to invite you, but they never returned from your realm. We assumed the worst." He gestured to the table where the fairies were seated. "Please join our celebration."

Millicent saw the pages scramble to set a place for her after Gillyfloss, and her eyes narrowed. "No!" she roared. "I will repay your insult with a prediction for your child."

Caroline tried to step in front of her baby but the fairy froze her with a gesture.

Millicent glowered at the smiling baby. "On her sixteenth birthday she will prick her finger on a spindle, and *die*."

The guests gasped in horror, and Talia began to wail. Millicent regarded the shocked faces, and cackled. She raised both hands, clicked her fingers, and vanished.

The room erupted into chaos. The queen picked up the bawling Talia and rocked her, but turned on her husband. "*This* is why you should beware of fairies!"

Then they noticed Gillyfloss standing in front of them. Caroline paled, and straightened as if expecting a blow.

Gillyfloss smiled. "You should not condemn all for the actions of one." The queen blushed, and Gillyfloss added, "I cannot undo the curse, but I can soften it. The only thing that can counteract hate is love."

Gillyfloss cupped her hands over the baby's head. "When you are sixteen you will prick your finger on a spindle, which will cause you to fall into an enchanted sleep for a hundred years. That spell will be broken by the kiss of true love."

The king and queen's strained smiles indicated they weren't convinced, but afterward Cecily congratulated Gillyfloss. "They don't understand the complex nature of magic," Cecily said to Gillyfloss. "That was a clever change,

but you will have to oversee this child for the next one hundred and sixteen years."

Gillyfloss shrugged, "I need a project."

Sure enough, Talia grew up to be pretty with good manners and a lovely singing voice. Gillyfloss visited often and encouraged the girl to read and study, although her father considered it a wasted effort. "Let her enjoy her time while she has it," he said once, when he was in a gloomy humor. Gillyfloss was determined to save the girl.

The king and queen ordered all the spindles in the kingdom burned, which caused much resentment among the people. Not everyone complied with the order. On the morning of Talia's sixteenth birthday, she chased her little dog into a dusty room in the highest reaches of the castle, and discovered an old woman using a spindle to spin thread.

Intrigued, Talia asked the dame about her task, for Talia had never seen a spindle, and knew nothing about the curse. The old lady offered to show Talia how to use it.

Within moments Talia pricked her finger. As the blood oozed out, an overwhelming fatigue possessed her, and she fell back into a chair. As her eyes closed, the old lady transformed into Millicent. Satisfied her curse had come into effect, she disappeared.

In that moment Gillyfloss entered the room. She had been preparing for sixteen years, for what she was about to do would require tremendous concentration. She sang a sleeping song. Every creature – the adults and children, the cats, dogs, mice, and horses – lay down and fell into a deep slumber. Then she changed the tune to one of fast growth.

Thick black brambles burst from the ground at the bottom of the castle walls, and grew at ferocious speed up the stone, over the gates, and covered all the windows. They were twenty feet deep, and the thorns were as tough as steel and as sharp as razors.

Gillyfloss set charms and ghostly sentinels about the castle so she would know if anyone attempted to enter. Many did, especially in the first decade, but none succeeded. The fairy tried to ease the suffering of those who had been cut off from their loved ones outside the charmed walls. "Magic is slippery," she sighed. One little boy called Phillip had been playing with his dog outside the castle walls when the spell came into effect and was left alone.

She ensured he was adopted into a happy and loving family. With her influence Phillip prospered, as did his children, and grandchildren. When the hundred-year mark approached, one of Phillip's great-great grandsons – a nobleman named Francis – was out hunting with his friend, Prince Simon. They stopped on a bluff overlooking the castle. Only the tops of the turrets were visible. Francis had grown up with stories about the Barred Castle since his family owned the land in the vicinity. He often came to gaze at it and dream up stories about its occupants.

Simon was fascinated. "Let's take a closer look," he said, digging his heels into his horse, and letting out a whoop. Francis galloped after him.

They jumped off their horses, and Simon inspected the barrier. "I'm surprised your family hasn't cut it down. With a number of strong men it would be a simple matter."

Francis restrained his irritation. "The best steel won't cut it, and it doesn't burn. Plus, there are the Haunts."

"Haunts?" Simon took an involuntary step back. Francis tried not to smile. Simon was easily spooked by stories of phantoms. "Ghosts patrol at night. Red-eyed and hungry. If you look upon them you go mad. If they touch you with their freezing hands your heart stops."

"Have you ever seen them?"

"I'm not mad, am I?" Francis noticed the lengthening shadows. "Let me show you the entrance."

They walked around the barrier until they came to a spot where they could just make out the castle gate.

Francis laid his hands upon a thick vine, and pressed close to get a good view. "The portcullis is up. We could walk in ... if we could pass these briars. And wake the sleeping princess."

"Princess?"

"That's the story. Inside is a princess waiting for a man of valor to wake her up."

"I'm valorous, and I'm a prince!"

Francis remained tight-lipped, recognizing the signs of one of Simon's infatuations. He knew better than to mention he had often dreamed of being the one to release the princess from the spell.

"But what if she's ugly?" Simon mused. "Or old?" He walked closer to the barrier. "That wouldn't be fair. There's no law that you must marry her, is there?"

The sun dipped below the horizon, and a strange sound shook the earth, as if the ground yawned. The briar in Francis's hand crumbled to dust.

Within seconds the entire barrier collapsed. Both men regarded the dark gate gaping in front of them. Bats flapped above their heads and a hunting owl shrieked. There were no clouds in the sky, and the crescent moon and stars offered some light, but the castle was thick with shadows. Simon stared about. "What about the ghosts? We should go and return with more men."

"I think it's safe. Don't you feel it? It's like we're being

**Gillyfloss set charms and ghostly sentinels about the castle.**

welcomed." Francis stepped forward. "We will be the first to enter in generations!"

They walked in carefully. At once they noticed dark forms on the ground. Simon seized Francis's arm. "Ghosts!"

They drew their swords but nothing happened. The shapes were people curled up on the ground, covered in leaves and dust. Francis knelt by one, brushed off a layer of dirt, and touched his skin. "He's warm, but not breathing."

Francis and Simon edged towards the steps that led to the main entrance.

It was darker inside. Clouds of dust were stirred up at each step. They coughed and their eyes watered.

Little swarms of fireflies flickered on and bobbed in front of them, guiding them in. They entered a great hall with a vaulted ceiling. Every footstep echoed. More forms slumped about the room, some sitting, others lying. A large platform dominated the hall, over which hung a canopy and garlands of dried flowers. The lights danced around it.

As the princes drew closer they saw someone lying on the platform. There was a glint of a crown on her head.

"The princess," Francis whispered.

Simon leaned closer, and recoiled instantly. The body was coated in a thick layer of cobwebs, as if she had been cocooned by a massive spider. "I want to leave, now," he said, too loudly. "We'll come back in daylight."

"No, we have to wake her!"

Simon stiffened. "Francis, I order you to leave with me."

A deeper silence grew as Francis stared at his friend. "I will meet you at home," he said, and turned his back on Simon to examine the dusty shape again.

Simon remained rooted to the spot by embarrassment.

Francis reached forward and peeled off ropes of thick web until a sleeping woman was revealed. Overcome by curiosity Simon peered over Francis's shoulder.

"As I guessed! She's withered."

Francis's voice was hushed, "Are you blind? She's radiant!"

"You've snorted too much dust. She's a crone with straw hair."

Francis bent closer, and Simon made a gagging noise.

"How do we wake you, princess?" Francis asked.

"Let her slumber, I say," Simon quipped.

The lights flickered and clustered above the princess's face. Francis tipped his head as if listening. He picked up her hand gently. "Wake up, m'lady," he said.

He touched her face with the back of his hand. "Please open your eyes."

Francis bent slowly, as if under a spell, and lightly brushed her lips with a kiss. He stood up, and rubbed her palm between his hands.

A sound, like a giant inhaled breath, filled the hall. Dozens of torches flared into life, and the fire in the great hearth sprung to life.

Dust and dirt fell from all the shapes, revealing King Augustus and Queen Caroline on their thrones, as well as soldiers, servants, guests, and hounds.

Talia's eyes opened. She gazed at Francis, and smiled. "I saw you in my dreams," she said. "You watched the castle, and imagined setting us free. Is it as you expected?"

"It is vastly better."

He helped her rise from her enchanted couch, and stood to one side as her mother and father rushed to embrace her.

Gillyfloss watched from the shadows and wiped away a tear. "Magic is slippery, but love is mighty."

# The Pied Piper of Hamelin

Hundreds of years ago, the town of Hamelin in Germany experienced an unusual problem: it was overrun by rats.

They scampered through attics and cellars, their claws clicking on wood and brick. They gnawed holes through walls and ate anything they could find. Every day the citizens of Hamelin opened their cupboards and discovered large, sleek rats sitting among their pots and pans, bold as brass and twice as cunning.

The rodents became so numerous and brave that they regularly cornered cats and dogs for fights. After the squealing, scratching, and howling died down, the rats always emerged victorious. The cats quit Hamelin to find easier living elsewhere, and the dogs slunk away at the sight of any of the large and dangerous vermin.

Traps didn't work for long, and the rats seemed to know what food was poisoned and avoided it — although many birds and other animals were not so lucky.

Mothers and fathers took turns to keep watch beside their children at night to ensure the rats would not scamper across the faces of their sleeping brood.

Finally, exasperated, the townsfolk demanded that the council of Hamelin take action immediately, or they would elect a new council.

The council of twelve and the Mayor met in their wood-panelled chamber and considered their options. They didn't have much money because the rats were ruining trade for the town, and all the rat-catchers they had employed so far had failed.

During their deliberations there was a light rap on the outside door. The steward opened it and was met by an extraordinary sight: a tall, thin man, wearing a pointed hat and dressed in a coat sewn from patches of colored and textured fabric, stood before him.

"Run along, fool," the steward said to the smiling man. "The council is meeting and is in no mood for entertainment or tricks."

The man bowed deeply to the steward and doffed his tapered hat. There were bells sewn into its point and they chimed merrily.

"Be so good as to introduce me to the council, for I am the legendary rat-catcher of Munich, and I can rid Hamelin of all your little troubles."

The steward believed his boast was worth taking a risk, and showed him in. The man stood before the council and declared, "I will remove the rats from your town in one day for the reasonable sum of a thousand florins."

The council members glanced at each other and raised their eyebrows, for they knew they couldn't pay such an enormous fee. On the other hand, none of them expected this jester dressed in pied clothing to perform the deed.

"Many have tried before you, young man," said the Mayor after a pause. "But if you are able to achieve this miracle, we will gladly pay your fee."

The man laughed. "You will see for yourself at noon tomorrow."

The innkeeper agreed to put the tall man up for the night. He was fed well and many people bought him beer that evening on the strength of what he claimed he would do.

The next morning a large crowd assembled by the clock tower in the square, for word of the promised feat had spread. The cheery man strolled from the inn and stood in the center of the people. With an elaborate gesture, a silver flute appeared in his hand. He proceeded to play it, his fingers flying across the holes, and a lively, enchanting tune emerged.

There was a rustling and high-pitched chittering, and men and women cried out: swarms of rats emerged from the surrounding houses. The sun shone on their brown coats, pink noses, and long tails. The townspeople pushed and shoved, and ran out of the way of the rodents.

The piper danced about as he played his bright tune, and soon he was encircled by the leaping, prancing creatures. Without a break in his playing, the piper began to move through the streets. People opened their shutters and doors and watched the rats dash out to join the swarm following the piper. Many folk clapped and cheered to the piper's tune.

He circled the town, picking up all the rats as he went, until his rat pack streamed after him. Then he played and capered his way down to the edge of the river Weser. He stepped nimbly onto a small rowing boat and pushed it away from the riverbank with his foot.

The rats splashed into the river, trying to pursue the piper. Some of them swam, but the weight of their brethren tumbling upon them pushed them under. The piper continued to play for an hour until all the rats drowned and were swept away from Hamelin by the current.

Finally, the piper could stop and return to land. The people cheered and applauded, and began celebrating the fact that the rodent curse had been lifted from their town.

The piper made his way to the town's council hall, where the council members had hastily assembled.

He bowed, his hat chiming, and said, "I have solved your problem. If you settle your debt, I shall take my leave. There are other towns in need of my skills."

The councillors feigned surprise, and the Mayor smiled. "If you produce a contract, of course we will honor it."

The piper's good cheer disappeared, and his features grew solemn. "We agreed on a price for my services, and now I have delivered. I expect payment immediately."

"And we never pay without a written contract," the Mayor replied.

The piper argued with them for some time, until the steward was ordered to remove the piper from their presence.

The piper banged his fist against the table. "Pay me as we agreed, or I will take from you something far more precious!"

"We do not respond to threats," the Mayor cried, and had the piper thrown out of the building.

The piper tried to explain to the people of Hamelin how their council had defaulted on his payment, but they were too busy partying to care.

After an hour of trying to be heard above the singing and merrymaking, the piper set his hat at a hard angle and marched out of the town gates.

That night, all the adults in the town drank and danced until the small hours, and fell into their beds happy and exhausted.

But as the dawn's blush lifted the dark of the night, a strange cajoling tune arose. The piper stood outside the gates, playing his silver pipe. Throughout the town, children woke and rubbed their eyes, but no adults stirred from their slumber. Girls and boys jumped out of their beds, and picked up those too young to walk. They ran out of their homes, still in their nightgowns, laughing and smiling at the beautiful tune.

One young boy, who had broken his leg a week earlier, struggled with his crutches and lagged behind the group of children. When they gathered by the town gates, the piper set off, dancing and playing, and all the children went after him, delighted.

Along the road they ran behind the piper, and up the trail that led through the forest to a great mountain. Straggling behind them on his crutches, the boy with the broken leg called out for them to wait, but they drew further and further away.

From a distance, the boy heard the piper's tune change, and a huge doorway opened in the rock face. Behind it shone a bright light, and he could just make out a scene of pastures and sun. The boy had never glimpsed anything so perfect in all his life. He redoubled his efforts to catch up with his friends, who were running through the door. But before he could join them, the massive door swung slowly shut with a final bang.

He spent the entire morning searching for a seam in the rock, and banging his fists against the unyielding surface.

Eventually he returned to the town. When he arrived, the place was in uproar. Everyone was screaming and crying. Mothers and fathers were searching everywhere for their beloved children.

When they saw the boy, they rushed to him to hear his story. Afterwards the town's soldiers took him back to the mountain on horseback, and spent all day and then all month searching for a way to open the door into the mountain.

No one ever saw the children of Hamelin again.

The boy's broken leg mended, but it is said that he heard the enticing piping in his dreams every night. Each day he returned to the mountain, desperate to be reunited with his friends and find his way to that blissful place he had once glimpsed.

Years later, he was discovered lying dead in the dewed grass by the mountain, with a contented smile on his face.

> Some of them swam, but the weight of their brethren tumbling upon them pushed them under.

# Pinocchio

In a small Italian town a carpenter named Maestro Antonio picked up a large piece of pinewood with the intention of carving it into a table leg. After he stripped off the bark, he lifted his chisel to begin the job, and heard a wee voice wail, "Be careful, don't hurt me!"

Maestro Antonio stood up and searched his workroom, wondering where the voice came from. He couldn't find anyone so he placed the chisel back on the wooden block. This time the voice giggled, "That tickles!"

He dropped the chisel. His father, also a carpenter, once warned him that every now and again a piece of wood would be more alive than others. "Those pieces have a special purpose," Antonio's father told him, "But they don't make good furniture."

Just at this moment his elderly neighbor Geppetto knocked on his door. Geppetto lived on his own, and was renowned for his grouchy nature. Even though he and Antonio quarrelled often, they remained friends.

After they said good morning to each other, Geppetto told Antonio he had a favor to ask: "I have decided to carve a beautiful wooden marionette. I can see it in my mind: it will be able to dance, fence, and turn somersaults. With such a character I would be able to tour around the world and earn a living. Do you have any suitable wood?"

At this the pinewood squeaked, "Bravo Geppetto!"

Geppetto smiled, for he thought it was his friend approving his plan. Antonio didn't correct him, for he realized instantly that the lively piece of wood was destined for Geppetto. He gave the pinewood to his friend with his blessings, and Geppetto went home to his cottage whistling merrily, imagining the fine future ahead of him.

Geppetto gathered his tools, sat on a chair in front of a bright fire, and sized the piece of wood. Before he started carving he decided to call the puppet Pinocchio, for he believed it was a lucky name.

He started shaping the head, and after he carved the eyes they began to blink and stare at him. Geppetto was startled, but he continued with the nose and mouth. Immediately Pinocchio began laughing, which irritated Geppetto. Finally, he ordered the puppet to be silent.

# Pinocchio

Pinocchio complied but stuck out his wooden tongue at Geppetto. When the old man carved his arms, Pinocchio immediately seized Geppetto's wig and threw it across the room.

At this Geppetto lost his temper. "Pinocchio!" he bellowed, "If you do not agree to behave I will leave you without any legs!"

"I'll be good," the puppet promised in a contrite voice. Grumbling, Geppetto fetched his wig, and finished carving Pinocchio.

As soon as Geppetto completed the last detail, Pinocchio leaped up and ran around the house, investigating everything and causing havoc. Soon Geppetto was red-faced and furious, but he wasn't quick enough to catch the nimble marionette. Within minutes Pinocchio unlatched the door and scampered out into the street, laughing and drawing a lot of attention. Geppetto ran after him, shouting.

Geppetto finally caught Pinocchio in the town square, but when his neighbors saw how roughly he handled the puppet they felt sorry for the little wooden boy. A policeman was summoned and hauled Geppetto off to jail.

Pinocchio ran through the town, peering in windows and making a nuisance of himself. When he got bored he scrambled through fields, chased butterflies, climbed trees, and eventually returned home at nightfall. Geppetto was still in jail so he had the house to himself.

Content with his day's adventures, Pinocchio threw himself into the chair by the fireplace. Suddenly he heard a strange chirping.

A little frightened, Pinocchio called out, "Who's there?"

A large, bright green cricket sat on the kitchen table. "I am the talking cricket and I've lived in this room for a hundred years," it said.

Pinocchio became a lot braver when he saw the insect. "Hop off bug!" he said rudely. "It's my home now."

"Not before I give you some advice," the cricket responded. Pinocchio sidled over to Geppetto's tools as the cricket spoke. "Woe betide boys who disobey their parents and run wild! They will never be happy for long, and—"

"With tomorrow's light I'm off to please myself! If I remain they'll put me in school all day, and where's the fun in that?" Pinocchio picked up Geppetto's hammer and eyed up the distance between him and the wise cricket.

"If you don't study and learn a trade you'll be another donkey-headed man braying in the street."

"I'll become the master of eating, drinking, and playing games!" Pinocchio declared. With that he threw the hammer at the cricket and smashed it dead. He scraped the green and red smear off the table and tossed it on the fire.

Pinocchio sat, crossed his feet in front of the flames, and fell asleep.

He woke up in the morning to the smell of smoke, and the yells of Geppetto, who had been released from prison earlier after a stern warning from the police to mind his temper.

Feeling groggy, Pinocchio looked up to see that his feet had burned off during the night! His legs now ended in two charred stumps. He couldn't escape when Geppetto berated him for his bad behavior. Eventually Geppetto questioned him about the absence of the cricket and Pinocchio told him the cricket had decided to leave. At this Pinocchio's nose grew an inch.

"Where did he go?" asked Geppetto, watching Pinocchio's face.

"He said he yearned to return to the forest of his youth," said Pinocchio. His nose extended by another inch. He pretended not to notice. "He wanted to have some excitement because you're so boring." At that lie, Pinocchio's nose grew several more inches.

Pinocchio now looked so ridiculous that Geppetto burst out laughing, which didn't please Pinocchio. He turned his head away to sulk and smashed the tip of his long nose against the wall. Pinocchio rested his long nose against the floorboards and regarded his burned ankles. He began to cry.

All mirth drained out of Geppetto, and love swelled in his heart instead. Geppetto had never had to take care of another person before, let alone a little boy, and for the first time he understood the grave responsibility. "*Please let me be able for the task*", he prayed. He sat down beside Pinocchio, hugged him, and told the puppet he would craft him new feet.

At that a soft light entered the room and a beautiful lady with blue hair and gossamer wings appeared. Both Geppetto and Pinocchio were struck dumb. Beside her was the ghost of the talking cricket. "Geppetto, your love will be rewarded if you stand by your son through thick and thin. Send him to school and watch over him. Pinocchio, if you care for your father one day you will become a real boy."

The fairy summoned a small flock of woodpeckers. They pecked Pinocchio's nose and within minutes it was back to its normal size. Pinocchio clapped his hands with joy.

The fairy left them with a final warning to be true to each other, and Geppetto set about carving new feet for Pinocchio. After they were done and attached to Pinocchio's legs, the man and the puppet danced together around the room.

Geppetto heeded the fairy's advice, and that day arranged for Pinocchio to enter school. Alas, he needed money for school books, but Geppetto was a poor man with no savings. He went to the pawn shop and sold his coat for the money. When Pinocchio saw him return, shivering, he asked, "Papa, where is your coat?"

Geppetto replied "It's nearly spring. Who needs a coat now?" and he set about making a meager meal for the two of them.

The following day Geppetto dressed Pinocchio in a new set of clothes he had spent the night sewing, and gave him the money for books. "Be good and learn," Geppetto told him, and sent him to school with a pat on his head.

For a time Pinocchio was an ideal son: he attended school, studied, and made friends. He felt like he was living the life of a real boy, and wondered when the fairy's prediction would come true. His best friend was named Romeo, but everyone called him Lamp-wick because he was tall and thin. Lamp-wick was quick with a joke, but he didn't enjoy the classroom, and often tried to persuade Pinocchio to skip school. Sometimes Pinocchio gave in and played truant with him. He'd learned not to lie to Geppetto, but also how to evade telling the truth. Geppetto, set in his ways, didn't always pay close enough attention to Pinocchio's activities.

One day on their walk home, Lamp-wick told Pinocchio he was leaving town for good.

"Where will you go and what will you do?" Pinocchio asked.

"I'm off to the Land of Toys, where boys play games and have fun morning to night." Lamp-wick explained. "There are no schools or teachers. Say, why don't you join me?"

Pinocchio heard a chirruping sound, and the ghost of the talking cricket appeared on his shoulder.

"Don't do it, Pinocchio," he warned. "You promised to heed your father and study."

Pinocchio ignored the cricket and walked with Lamp-wick, listening to his description of the wonders of the

> "I'm off to
> the Land of Toys,
> where boys play games
> and have fun morning
> to night."

Land of Toys. He remembered what it was like to run about as he pleased with no one to tell him what to do.

They stopped at the outskirts of the town, and Lamp-wick let out a whoop and pointed to a large wagon rumbling down the street, driven by twelve donkeys. "That's it, Pinocchio!" he shouted. The driver pulled up beside them. There were ten boys inside singing and laughing. One of them opened the door, and Lamp-wick jumped in.

"Is it true?" Pinocchio asked the driver, who was a small, round man. "You're taking them to the Land of Toys. And they can play all day?"

"Yes, every boy can do as he wishes." One of the donkeys kicked at his traces, and the driver struck him with his stick. "Be quiet!" he yelled at the poor beast, and it trembled in pain and fear. A tear rolled down its nose. Pinocchio rubbed its head to calm it.

He heard a voice whisper, "Stupid boy, you'll be very sorry if you leave."

Thinking it was the ghost of the talking cricket, Pinocchio bristled. "I'm not stupid!" he declared. At that, he jumped into the wagon. All the boys cheered. The driver cracked his whip across the ears of the donkeys and they sprang into a trot. Pinocchio didn't have time to feel bad, for his new friends were full of entertaining stories. At some point they all fell asleep as the wagon rolled across hills and through villages.

The next morning they arrived at the Land of Toys, which had a giant entrance in the shape of a laughing

Pinocchio

mouth. The boys leapt off the wagon and sprinted across the threshold. Inside were carnival rides, gaming halls, candy stalls, soda pop fountains, and lots of boys running about madly, shouting and playing. There were cabins if they wanted to sleep, but no one told anyone what to do or what schedule to keep.

Pinocchio and Lamp-wick had more fun in a week than they thought was possible in a year. When they rolled out of bed one afternoon, Pinocchio noticed something strange. Lamp-wick had a pair of donkey ears growing from his head.

Pinocchio dragged him to a mirror and showed him. Lamp-wick turned pale with fright.

"What's happening? ... *Hee haw!*" Lamp-wick clapped his hands over his mouth, his eyes round like saucers. "I ... sound like a donkey!" he gasped. He pointed at Pinocchio, and gestured to the looking glass.

Pinocchio gazed into it and saw a pair of sleek donkey ears sprouting from his head. His jaw dropped open. Then he twitched his ears, and burst out laughing... until it turned into a bout of donkey braying.

From around them arose the sound of panicked boys crying and braying. All the friends they made on that fateful trip to the Land of Toys were changing into donkeys.

Pinocchio and Lamp-wick bolted out of their cabin, but within minutes they lost control of their legs, and collapsed to the ground, twitching.

Pinocchio dragged him to a mirror and showed him. Lamp-wick turned pale with fright.

"Help! *Hee haw!*" yelled Lamp-wick. That was the last human sound he made. Bones creaked and popped, and hair sprouted all over his body. He screamed in agony as his nose and chin extended and merged to create a muzzle. He flipped on his side, and wobbled up on his legs a few mintues later as a sturdy grey donkey.

Terrified, Pinocchio tried to call out for Geppetto, the talking cricket, or the fairy with the blue hair, but all that came out was an awful braying.

A coating of hair erupted all over his body. His legs and arms changed shape, and joints contorted. His fingers clenched into fists and merged, his feet contracted and flattened until they became four hooves.

His face elongated, his jaw and teeth morphed, and his eyesight changed. A tail grew and he lashed it about, unsure how to control it. Finally, he lay on his side as a brown donkey, his four legs quivering, and he didn't know how to get up or communicate with anyone.

Around him all the boys were donkeys, braying in distress, some on the ground, and other trotting about or bucking their back legs furiously as if they could kick off their new bodies.

The short round man who had driven them to the Land of Toys arrived, with his stick stuck in his belt and his whip in his hand. He regarded the dozen donkeys and grinned.

With cracks from his whip he forced all the former boys

to stand up, and drove them into a large stable at the rear of the Land of Toys. As they jostled in, Pinocchio noticed a new cohort of boys had arrived. He tried to cry out to warn them, but hee-hawed instead. The boys laughed at the donkeys and ran off to have fun.

Pinocchio and Lamp-wick were put in a stall together. The man took a currycomb from his pocket and brushed their coats until they shone like silk. Next he bridled them, and brought them to market.

Within an hour Lamp-wick was purchased by a farmer whose donkey had died the day before. The farmer dragged Lamp-wick away, who brayed piteously with big tears rolling down his fuzzy muzzle. Pinocchio could not break free to comfort his friend. The owner of a circus spotted Pinocchio's spirited struggle, and thought he would be perfect for an act at the circus. Within minutes Pinocchio's sale was arranged, and he was led to their campsite.

His new master pushed him into a small stable and put hay into the manger. Pinocchio tried it and spat it out because of the terrible taste. At this his owner unfurled his whip and lashed him across the back. "Obstinate donkey! You'll eat what I give you, or you'll get nothing at all."

By nightfall, Pinocchio the donkey decided hay wasn't so bad.

The next day Pinocchio's master brought him into the circus ring to begin his training. He wanted Pinocchio to dance to music, stand on his back legs on a ball, and jump through flaming hoops. Pinocchio was not yet used to his donkey body and found it hard to learn all the maneuvers. Whenever he made a mistake he was lashed. It took him three months, and many beatings, to learn the entire routine perfectly. During this period the circus traveled from town to town, so Pinocchio never knew where he was. At night, in his stall, alone and hurt, he yearned to be home with his father.

Finally the day arrived for Pinocchio's first performance. The Ring-Master announced him, and Pinocchio trotted out to the roar of the crowd and the glare of the lights. He wore a new bridle of leather with polished brass buckles, red silk ribbons braided into his mane, with a sash of gold and silver fastened around his neck.

His owner cracked his whip and Pinocchio knelt on his two front legs to bow to the audience. He began his routine: trotting, galloping, and performing tricks on command. At one point as he looked up Pinocchio thought he glimpsed Geppetto in the audience. He stopped suddenly and began braying at Geppetto, but his owner struck him on the nose with the handle of his whip and Pinocchio's eyes streamed with tears. When he'd stopped crying, Geppetto was gone.

Disconsolate, Pinocchio could not concentrate on the routine. When it came to jumping through the flaming hoops he fumbled and struck his legs against a hoop, which fell off its stand and rolled, burning, towards the audience. A stampede of people erupted out of the tent, and Pinocchio could barely walk back to his stable on his sore legs, despite the thrashing the Ring Master rained on him.

A vet was called to tend to Pinocchio's wounds, but she declared that the donkey would be lame for life. Pinocchio's master immediately handed Pinocchio's reins to the stable boy and ordered him to sell the donkey. "What use is he now?" he exclaimed, and turned away.

Pinocchio was led, hobbling, to the market again. This time no one showed any interest in a lame donkey. At last a drum maker decided to purchase him. "I'll skin him and make a drum from him," the man said. Pinocchio tried to escape but he was too lame to run.

The drum maker dragged Pinocchio to the top of a small cliff overlooking the sea. He tied a rope and a large rock around Pinocchio's neck, and threw him over the edge, hoping to drown Pinocchio.

Pinocchio splashed into the water and sank quickly, thrashing his legs in terror. Just at this moment, he saw an enormous shark swimming toward him.

With one snap it bit through the rope and swallowed Pinocchio whole. As Pinocchio passed through its row of serrated teeth, the donkey skin was slashed right off Pinocchio's hard body. He landed with a clatter of wooden limbs in the middle of the shark's cavernous belly. He was no longer a donkey but still a pinewood marionette.

"That was lucky!" Pinocchio said, but when he looked

**With one snap it bit through the rope and swallowed Pinocchio whole.**

around he realized he was caught in a new dilemma. He noticed a small fishing boat in the middle of the shark's stomach. "Hello!" he called out.

A welcome face popped up from the boat: it was Geppetto! For a moment neither of them could believe it. Father and son embraced, and cried tears of joy. Later, they settled back and related their adventures. Geppetto described how he had followed rumors of Pinocchio's whereabouts for months, until, in despair, he even went to a circus act that featured a donkey called Pinocchio.

"That was me!" Pinocchio said, and told his father about his cruel treatment at the circus.

Geppetto explained how after the circus trip the fairy visited and told him that if he was willing to take a dangerous sea voyage he and Pinocchio would be reunited.

"And so we are!" declared Pinocchio, and they hugged again.

"Now we have to escape this beast's belly," Geppetto said.

Since Pinocchio was made of wood, he was sure that his father would be able to cling to him like a raft as they swam to shore. "But how can we get *out* of the shark?" Geppetto asked.

They searched Geppetto's boat for supplies, in the hopes that they would find something useful. Between them they decided to use a can of pepper and the smoke from a burning torch to force the shark to expel them.

Pinocchio held the can of pepper and looked up at his father who was lighting the torch. "What if it doesn't work?"

Geppetto patted Pinocchio's wooden head and smiled. "Together we will find another way."

Carefully, they climbed out of the stomach and along the shark's throat. As they peeked up into the shark's massive mouth, they saw it snap up a school of shining fish, which landed bloodied and flipping inside.

"Watch out, it's going to swallow!" Geppetto shouted, and he thrust his burning torch against the shark's gums. Pinocchio took off the lid of the pepper can and threw it into the air.

The great shark convulsed, dove upwards, and opened its mouth to soothe the pain. Gallons of sea water rushed in. Geppetto caught hold of a fishing pole wedged between two of the shark's giant teeth, and grabbed Pinocchio's arm as he was swept back into the stomach.

The shark broke the surface of the water and leaped in a marvelous arc over the waves. Geppetto saw his chance. He swung on the fishing pole, and flung Pinocchio and himself out between the shark's jaws. They sailed through the air and landed in the churning sea. They heard a deafening roar as the shark landed, and a huge swell of water caught them and carried them a long distance. Geppetto and Pinocchio kept a firm grip on each other as they bobbed and gasped in the water.

It was dawn, and they could make out the cliff in the distance. Pinocchio began swimming strongly to the shore. He was naturally buoyant, but Geppetto was an elderly man who had already been taxed beyond his strength.

Pinocchio urged him on, saying "Not long now, Papa!", and telling him to hang onto him as Pinocchio's arms spun in clean strokes through the water.

They were still far from the shore when Geppetto's arms slipped from around Pinocchio's neck for the first time. Pinocchio struggled to keep him afloat. After all his trials even sturdy Pinocchio was exhausted.

He offered up a prayer to the fairy with the blue hair: *Please m'am, save my father.* It seemed to Pinocchio that as he gulped and swam with his father on his back, he saw her familiar glow light up the seafoam.

*What about you, Pinocchio?* He heard her ask.

*Please keep Geppetto safe. That's my only desire.*

*As you wish,* she said.

A moment later he heard a squeaking sound, and the nose of a dolphin broke the surface in front of him. Pinocchio used the last of his failing strength to place his father on the dolphin's back. He watched as it carried his father swiftly to the shore.

Pinocchio tried to keep up, but his arms felt like lead. He slipped under the surface and plummeted to the bottom of the sea.

When Geppetto came to, he was in the shallows of the beach, as far as the dolphin could bring him. He stood, shakily, the small waves pushing at his legs.

A terrible realization dawned on him. "Pinocchio!" he

screamed, and lunged back into the sea.

The dolphin swam in front of him, barring his way. At that moment he saw another dolphin slicing through the water, with Pinocchio on his back.

Geppetto gently took his son from the dolphin, and hugged him to his chest.

"Wake up Pinocchio!" he pleaded.

But Pinocchio did not wake up.

Later that night, Geppetto sat vigil beside the bed where he had laid Pinocchio. He had found a kind fisherwoman who was willing to take them in, and give them the use of a bedroom.

Pinocchio appeared like an ordinary puppet. None of the magic that had kept him animated remained. It had been lost to the sea.

Geppetto held his son's hand and raised it to his cheek. He remembered how the boy infuriated him at first. "Pinocchio," he whispered, "please forgive me. I should have been more patient. I should have been a better father." He wept inconsolably.

He turned to stoke the meager fire and add another log. The warmth and light increased, but when he turned from

his task he realized that it wasn't the fire. The fairy with the blue hair was in the room by Pinocchio's bed.

She smiled down at the pinewood marionette and touched his chest. A glow suffused his little wooden frame.

"Wake up Pinocchio," she said. "You and your father need each other."

Pinocchio's eyes fluttered open. He was no longer made of wood and wire, but of flesh and blood.

He sat up in bed, and gazed at the beautiful fairy. "Thank you," he said. He noticed the ghost of the talking cricket, looking down at him from a shelf.

"I'm sorry I killed you," he added. Now he experienced being a real boy, Pinocchio truly appreciated the value of all life.

Pinocchio laughed at the wonder of it all, and opened his arms to his father.

Geppetto ran to his son, and hugged him tight.

# The Master and His Apprentice

Luke came from a long line of goat herders. His father had been a goat herder, just like his father before him, but at the age of twelve Luke decided to break from family tradition. He yearned for the adventure, fame, and fortune enjoyed by heroes in stories, not a quiet life in a backwater village. So he took it upon himself to learn his letters and numbers from Brother Martin, the monk who lived in a monastery in their hamlet.

Several miles north, on the road to the city, rose an impressive stone keep. In it dwelled a mysterious gentleman, whom the villagers referred to as "Master Drake". He visited their village to buy supplies, and rode a majestic black stallion. Luke spied on him at every opportunity.

There were dark rumors about the nature of Master Drake's business. Many claimed to have observed strange lights and odd noises coming from his dwelling late at night. Angus, the village's chief drunk — their village had many drunks — claimed that one dark moon he had seen Master Drake on his horse in a field speaking to the queen of a vast, shining fairy host. Brother Martin always blessed himself at the mention of Drake's name, and stopped any conversation about "that wicked man".

After weeks of internal debate, Luke considered his opportunity for glory would be much improved if he took service with Master Drake, despite the chance of perdition. He washed his face, put on his cleanest garments, kissed his mother farewell, and made his way to Drake's keep.

The square stone tower stood inside a walled courtyard. Beside the large oak entrance was a heavy iron door bell with a chain. Luke rang it three times before the door creaked open to reveal a thin, elderly man with a sour expression.

"I wish to speak to Master Drake," Luke announced boldly.

The man raised an eyebrow, but his elaborate wave of the hand to permit him entry implied mockery. Luke gritted his teeth and marched into the cobblestone courtyard.

The man led Luke into the tower at a leisurely pace, up two floors via a cramped stone stairway, and into a big room lined with books from floor to ceiling. Master Drake stood by a plinth, on which rested a huge, open tome. He didn't look up from his reading when they entered. After indicating that Luke should stand in front of Master Drake, the man swiftly left the room.

"Thank you, Danvers," said Master Drake, and turned his attention to Luke.

For a moment, when the force of Master Drake's regard rested on him, Luke thought it would be best to run away from that place forever and accept his lot as a goat herder. Instead, he opened his mouth to speak.

"You're late," Master Drake snapped.

Luke blinked, confused. "How can I be late when I wasn't expected?"

"I've been expecting you for a week. What took you so long?" Master Drake sniffed. "And you must bathe instantly. A good olfactory sense is imperative in this undertaking, and unless you wash you'll never smell anything other your own wretched stench. Danvers!" he yelled. "Inform Mrs. Shaw to boil water for the apprentice's first bath. She'll require an entire cake of soap."

Throughout the tirade, Luke stood, his mouth agape. All his careful arguments about why Master Drake should take him into service were for naught.

"I have bathed before," Luke said hotly.

"But not recently."

A deep crimson flushed Luke's cheeks.

Master Drake closed the tome in front of him. It was covered in black leather with dark iron corners, and had a huge clasp and lock. He drew an iron key from a ring of keys on his belt and locked the book shut. A thick chain bound the book to the plinth.

"Your contract is on the bench," he said, pointing to a long, sturdy table that was scorched in places. On it rested vials, herbs, colored string, powders, candles, and a page of parchment written in ink.

Master Drake strode across to the bench, the keys jangling at his waist, picked up a quill from an ink pot, and pushed it at Luke. "Sign it, now!"

Luke took the quill and craned his neck to read.

Master Drake waved his hand in a dismissive fashion. "Just sign it."

Luke scowled. "Not before I read it."

A slight touch of amusement softened Master Drake's features. "Quite right. Never enter any arrangement without understanding the terms and conditions. Especially when the contact runs for ten years."

Luke tried to restrain his gulp.

Ten years!

When Luke finally signed his name, not without trepidation, Master Drake clapped his hands and grinned.

"Let's get started."

Every night for the next three years, Luke's daily routine remained the same: his day started at dawn, cleaning out the stables and brushing down Midnight, Master Drake's stallion. Then he had to wash and eat breakfast with Mrs. Shaw in the kitchen before the first round of studies. Master Drake schooled him in Latin,

> "I've been expecting you for a week. What took you so long?"

French, history, politics, and literature. After a light repast, the afternoon was taken up with exercises set by Master Drake and any chores that Mrs. Shaw saw fit to assign him. The evening was set aside for music and reading. There were days when the boy could barely pull himself up the narrow stone staircase to his bed.

As time wore on, Luke became impatient with the hard work and constant lessons with no mystery or excitement. Most of all Luke longed to open Master Drake's great grimoire bound in black calfskin.

One day Master Drake received an urgent message, after which he disappeared into his study for a long period. Later, he whirled out of the room shouting orders, and within an hour he galloped out of the keep on Midnight, with Danvers beside him on another horse.

Mrs. Shaw saw the grin on Luke's face and immediately set him to work scrubbing the large dining room on the ground floor. He huffed and grumbled to himself as he labored away. After fetching and emptying two heavy buckets of water from the well, he sat on his heels and noticed how much he still had to clean. Luke threw down the brush in disgust. He deserved a break.

He crept into the study very quietly. Clouds of dust floated in the beam of sunshine, illuminating the room. Then the realization hit him like a thunderbolt. The grimoire — "the heart of dark secrets", Master Drake once called it — was open.

Luke edged closer, looking over his shoulder. The pages were not written in any language he'd been taught, and strange symbols decorated the edges. He found one phrase that seemed familiar, and rolled the words through his mind. Then with a confident gesture he spoke the foreign words.

Nothing happened. Disappointed, Luke repeated the words, louder, and then again a third time.

The room shook slightly and a noxious smell pervaded the space. Suddenly a huge beast squatted in front of Luke. It looked like a gigantic goat with coal-black hair. A massive set of curling horns adorned its head, and large bat wings protruded from its back. Its orange eyes blazed with fury.

"What is your bidding?" it asked in a deep, resonant voice.

Panicked, Luke's mind went blank.

"Boy, if you do not give me an order, I will find something else to do!" It regarded him with malign interest.

The silence was broken with Mrs. Shaw yelling from the kitchen. "Luke, have you finished yet?"

Luke stared at the beast. "Bring me buckets of water to wash the floor downstairs," he blurted.

The creature snorted derisively. "As you bid, so shall it be," it said, then vanished.

Luke sped down the staircase and burst into the room as a bucket of water floated in, sloshing with water. It tossed the water on the floorboards, sending suds streaming. Luke laughed, delighted. The bucket floated back out to the well, then returned after a few moments brimming with water, which was thrown onto the floor.

After the tenth bucket of water, Luke woke from his daze of wonder. "Stop!" he called out. "I bid you stop!"

The goat's face shimmered in the ankle-deep water.

"Those are not the right words to send me away," it declared. The bucket began refilling quickly, and more buckets flew in, ever faster, bringing water to flood the room.

Mrs. Shaw cried out in anger from below as water poured into the kitchen. Luke ran upstairs to the book, but he couldn't decide which phrase to pick. With a sickening lurch in his stomach, he realized he could make things worse. When he went back to the stairs, the water lapped halfway up the steps. The room below him was filled!

Never had he been so desperate to see Master Drake's stern face. Instead he heard only the dreadful gloating of the demon, and rushing water filling the keep.

Just as the water touched the threshold of the study, a shout rang out so loud that the stones trembled. Luke wondered what new horror awaited him. In an instant, the water vanished. Luke picked his way down the slippery steps.

Master Drake stood in the hallway, wearing a murderous expression. Beside him stood Mrs. Shaw, her clothes soaking wet. Before Luke could explain, Master Drake spoke.

"You ill-disciplined child! Get to your room this instant."

Luke fled from the terrible contempt in his voice.

*A* week later Luke was summoned to Master Drake's study.

The great black book lay open, and the master stood by it. His expression was somber.

"You've had time to ponder what happened. Your words will now determine how, or if, we progress together."

Luke nodded.

"What have you learned?"

"That I have the barest grasp of the workings of the world." They were bitter words to say. "That what we do is no game, and that people can be hurt if our actions are taken lightly."

"Indeed, and it is well that you acknowledge it." Master Drake remained silent for a while and gazed out the window. "Anything else?" he added.

"That you left the book open on purpose to test me. And I failed you." Luke could not bear to look at his teacher's face.

"It is only failure if we learn nothing from our mistakes. Come here."

Luke approached the tome carefully.

Master Drake tapped the page. "Today's lesson: banishing. Let us begin."

# The Goose Girl

In a remote kingdom far to the south, a queen reigned and brought up her only daughter. Many years previously, Princess Roselyn had been promised in marriage to Prince Cosmo, who lived in a distant land. When she turned eighteen, Roselyn faced a long journey away from her home and her mother for the first time.

The Queen assembled her daughter's dowry with a heavy heart, for she was loath to part with her only child. She ensured that Roselyn would have the finest treasures to bring with her and remind her of her childhood home. The Queen also recognized that Roselyn was a quiet and gentle girl, and ill-equipped to cope with hard circumstances. So she retired to her private chamber and cut her hand with a knife. A row of scarlet beads sprang up from the shallow incision. She shook her hand over a linen handkerchief until three drops of blood fell upon it. The Queen's family had always known charms and spells, and the Queen had passed some of that knowledge to her daughter.

She returned to Roselyn's bedroom, where the chambermaid, Joan, was helping Roselyn pack. She handed her daughter the handkerchief.

"Keep this upon you at all times," she said, "for it will offer you protection on your journey." Roselyn tucked it inside her dress next to her skin.

The Queen then commanded Joan to accompany her young mistress and keep her safe. Joan had not expected to leave her home and her family, so she was not pleased, but she curtsied and swore to the Queen that she would protect Roselyn always.

As a final gift, the Queen gave Roselyn her favorite horse, named Falada, who could speak when it moved him to do so. The Queen said goodbye to her daughter in the castle courtyard, her eyes red from private tears, for she did not want to display her true grief in front of the court or her daughter.

Roselyn and Joan rode out on their horses, accompanied by a regiment of the Queen's best soldiers. A week into their journey, the group was attacked by bandits. Amid the chaos of the battle, and despite her great fear, Roselyn managed to escape with Joan and gallop away from the screams and clang of swords. They had little of Roselyn's dowry with them, but they were grateful to be alive and free.

As they made their way towards their new home, Joan asked Roselyn questions about her bridegroom. She realized that the couple had not seen each other in years, and their only communication had been through letters. A plan began to form in her mind, but she was aware of the protection provided by the Queen's blood, and Falada's powers.

At one point, tired and thirsty, Roselyn asked Joan to fetch her some water from a nearby stream.

"I am not your slave," Joan answered haughtily. "Get your own drink."

Roselyn was too timid to rebuke Joan, so she dismounted Falada, knelt on the riverbank, and cupped her hands to drink. At that moment she felt the folded handkerchief warm against her skin, and a voice said, "If your mother knew of this, her heart would break in two."

Roselyn climbed back on Falada and continued their journey. Later, she became hungry and asked Joan for some apples from their meager supplies.

Joan sneered at Roselyn with an expression of disdain. "Are you crippled? Get them yourself."

Threatened by Joan's fierce demeanor, Roselyn slowed Falada and reached into the saddlebags on Joan's horse. She took out two pink apples, but as she urged her horse forward again Joan grabbed the best apple from Roselyn's hand and bit into it. Roselyn's handkerchief warmed and she heard a whisper: "If your mother knew of this, her heart would break in two."

That afternoon they stopped by a small pool. They guessed that Prince Cosmo's castle had to be nearby, and Roselyn wished to wash so that she would be presentable to her fiancé and his family. They tied the horses to a tree and descended to the rocks by the shining water. Roselyn asked Joan to help her undress, but she replied with scorn.

"Are you a child? Do it yourself."

Roselyn struggled to unlace her dress, and as she did so the handkerchief became heated and said, "If your mother knew of this, her heart would break in two." Roselyn stepped out of her gown and knelt by the water.

In that moment, Joan swooped up the handkerchief, wrapped it around a rock and threw it into the pool. It sank to the bottom immediately. She then pulled a dagger from a secret sheath in her boot and pressed its keen blade against Roselyn's neck. Joan threatened to kill Roselyn unless the girl agreed to swap places with her and swear

*If your mother knew of this, her heart would break in two.*

under the open sky that she would never reveal what had happened.

Roselyn saw the conviction in Joan's eyes and her sure grip on the dagger. Fearful for her life, she made the promise and put on Joan's clothes. When they returned to the horses, Joan climbed into Falada's saddle. The horse swung his great head around to look, but she hid her face and remained quiet.

Joan and Roselyn arrived at the castle to great fanfare and celebration. Prince Cosmo and his parents assumed that Joan was the Princess. She told them of the bandit attack and embellished the story greatly so that she became the saviour of a poor servant girl. Prince Cosmo's eyes shone with pride, and Joan was swept into the household to be pampered and cared for.

Roselyn stayed outside, unsure what to do. Looking out of a window, the King noticed Roselyn's poise and beauty, and asked Joan about her. She suggested that the King find her some work. The King had few positions available, but he needed someone to help a young boy, called Conrad, tend the castle's geese.

Roselyn was given a small room to share with other young servant girls, and every day she had to drive the geese past the stables, through a dark gateway in the castle's walls, and out to a pasture by a pond. Sometimes she could glimpse Falada and it brightened her mood. The geese were large and unpredictable, and if they snapped at her with their great beaks, it left awful bruises.

Conrad liked Roselyn a little too well, and she was always trying to find excuses to keep as far from him as possible when they worked together.

Whenever she saw Joan walk by laughing with her new husband, Roselyn's heart despaired. At night, lying awake in the dark and listening to the snores of the castle's maids, the Princess would think of her mother and the terrible secret she had sworn to uphold.

Joan had not forgotten Roselyn or Falada, for she was determined never to lose her new position. One day, she asked Prince Cosmo a favor:

"Could you have the horse named Falada sent to the saddle maker's yard? He is an ill-tempered steed and nearly foiled my escape from the bandits."

The prince issued the order happily.

Roselyn was heartbroken when she heard of Falada's dreadful fate. She scraped together the few coins she had earned in the hope of saving Falada, but by the time she arrived at the saddle maker's yard, the deed had been done. Instead, Roselyn gave the money to the saddle maker's helper and asked him to preserve and nail Falada's head in the dark gateway, so she could look upon him as she drove the geese past.

> Roselyn saw the conviction in Joan's eyes and her sure grip on the dagger.

From then on, Roselyn walked under Falada in the shadows of the gateway twice a day. His empty eye sockets and bared teeth glistened in the low light, and he would whisper gently:

"Alas, young queen, passing through,

If your mother knew of this,

Her heart would break in two."

It made Roselyn's life a little more bearable to see her old friend, despite her grief. Conrad often questioned her about the horse and the strange words, but she shrugged her shoulders and pretended not to understand.

In the meadow by the pond, while the geese wandered about honking and pecking for food, the Princess would untie her golden braid and comb it out. Sometimes she would recite a tune her mother used to sing while she braided Roselyn's hair as a child. Conrad usually ruined this moment of peace because he admired her shining locks, and pestered her to give him a few strands of her hair. Roselyn always refused, since her mother had taught her never to gift anyone with her hair for fear that he would use it to cast a spell upon her. Instead she sang a little song:

"Blow, wind, blow,

Catch Conrad's hat,

So he must chase it,

Until I braid my hair,

And tie it up anew."

With that, a breeze would spring up and pluck Conrad's hat from his head, so that he was forced to run far and wide to retrieve it. Always, by the time he returned, red-faced and sweaty, Roselyn had pinned up her braid again.

This happened so often that Conrad's desire for Roselyn turned into resentment and anger at her ability to avoid his advances. One day, the King was passing by the meadow, and Conrad was again frustrated after chasing his hat all afternoon. He bowed and asked for the King's attention. The King was surprised by Conrad's forceful interruption, but indicated that he should speak.

Conrad complained bitterly about the goose girl, saying that she was lazy and left him to do all the work. The King raised his eyebrows at this, for his steward kept him well informed of all the goings-on in this household, and he had heard nothing but good reports about the young woman. On the other hand, the reason Conrad had been given the duty of herding the geese was because of his persistent idleness.

Sensing disbelief from the King, the boy also related the mysterious words spoken by the dead horse and Roselyn's ability to conjure up a wind. Intrigued, the King dismissed Conrad and told him that he would investigate further.

The next day, the King dressed plainly and followed Roselyn and Conrad. In the shadow of the gateway's low arch, he heard the shriveled head of the dead horse whisper to Roselyn:

"Alas, young queen, passing through,

If your mother knew of this,

Her heart would break in two."

The King shivered at the ghostly words, but went after the two servants. He hid nearby and saw Conrad attempt to get close to Roselyn, and how she edged away from him. She let down her glorious waves of hair and Conrad tried to sneak up and grab her. Roselyn sang out:

"Blow, wind, blow,

Catch Conrad's hat,
So he must chase it,
Until I braid my hair,
And tie it up anew."

The wind seized Conrad's hat and it swiftly wheeled away from him. The King found it hard not to laugh at Conrad's wild sprint in pursuit of his hat. And an awful suspicion began to form in the King's mind, for there had always been rumors about his in-law's unnatural abilities.

Back at the castle, the King summoned Roselyn to his study and questioned her about her past. Her answers were evasive, and in the end he told her what he had witnessed earlier.

"I cannot explain to you or anyone else my sorrows," she replied, "for I was forced to take an oath of secrecy under pain of death."

The King assessed the young woman in front of him, and advised her to speak her secrets to the iron stove in his room to relieve her pain. With that, he left the room and went to the neighbouring room, through which the stovepipe ran.

Roselyn was glad for an excuse to unburden herself. In a low voice, she recounted to the stove what had happened on their journey, and the awful fraud that Joan had committed. The King heard everything and alternated between being furious at Joan's duplicitous nature and marveling at Roselyn's fortitude and integrity.

He immediately summoned Roselyn and informed her that he knew everything. The Princess was taken to one of the most beautiful rooms in the castle, and bathed and dressed in a gown embroidered with flowers. The King took Prince Cosmo aside and related the entire story. Cosmo seethed with anger at the betrayal, and also blamed himself for not noticing the differences between the woman who presented herself to his court and the woman who had written to him for years.

That night, they arranged a grand banquet, and Prince Cosmo sat beside his false bride. Roselyn was seated at the end of the table, but Joan didn't recognize her because she was so radiant and happy.

After food and wine had been consumed, the Prince told Joan a story of a woman who had attempted to fool the throne and steal from another.

"What punishment would you inflict upon this devious person, my dear?" he asked.

Joan sipped wine and searched her cruel heart for an answer.

"Strip her bare and place her in a barrel studded with sharp nails inside. Hitch two white horses to the barrel and have them roll the barrel through the city until she is dead."

The room fell silent at her terrible suggestion.

The King stood up and regarded Joan gravely. "You have pronounced your own punishment," he declared. He gestured to the soldiers and they dragged her away.

Roselyn couldn't find it in her heart to rejoice at Joan's sentence, and she refused to watch it being carried out, but Joan's screams could be heard from the highest turret, and it is said that it took ten men to scrub her blood from the cobbled streets.

After a time, Cosmo gained Roselyn's trust and affection, and they were married. Their wedding parade through the cheering city was led by a flock of snow-white geese.

# The Island of Skeletons

**B**ig Wave was a fearless hunter and warrior, but he was defenseless when a plague ravaged the people of his tribe. The only other survivors were his nephew, Red Shell, and his niece, Wild Sage, the children of his sister. Big Wave and the children left the silent longhouses of their village, and searched for a new place to live.

They discovered their new home at the edge of a forest, with a vast lake nearby and plenty of game. Working together, they built an elm bark longhouse. Wild Sage was older than Red Shell, and often acted like his mother, which led to arguments. Red Shell loved to spend his days hunting and fishing with his uncle, and resented being left at home with his sister. One winter morning, Big Wave insisted Red Shell remain behind while he foraged. Snow blanketed the ground and Big Wave knew he could hunt faster if the boy wasn't with him. Red Shell, cooped up and sulking, started a fight with Wild Sage who wanted him to help her scrape deerskin hides.

Red Shell left in a huff, taking his bow, determined to prove himself. When the sun edged the earth Red Shell returned cold, embarrassed, and empty-handed. He discovered the entrance to the longhouse smashed, as if a huge creature had battered it open. Inside, everything was destroyed, and Wild Sage was missing.

Big Wave returned, and examined the tracks around the longhouse. The massive footsteps indicated a giant had taken Wild Sage. They sped along the trail to the lake, where it looked like the giant and Wild Sage left in a canoe.

Man and boy were devastated. Over the following weeks they searched for Wild Sage, but found no trace. Red Shell took it badly. He threw himself into practicing with his bow, learning to fight, and becoming adept at tracking and hunting. To protect his nephew, Big Wave drew a large circle of sacred maize around the longhouse as a barrier to the giant. He warned Red Shell never to cross the magic line when alone.

Red Shell obeyed his uncle initially, but by summer the days were long and he longed for new sights. He left the circle and visited the lake. He threw pebbles into the water and shot arrows.

All at once, a voice hailed him. "Are you as good with that bow when you are shooting against a person?"

Red Shell turned to see a tall, smiling man, holding a bow. The stranger challenged Red Shell to discover who could shoot the furthest. The boy welcomed the chance to show off. Indeed, he beat the man.

The man laughed, taking his loss well. "Are you as good a swimmer?" So the two of them swam while holding their breath, and once again Red Shell was the victor. The man shook his head in amazement. "As a reward I'll take you to an island in the lake, where there are many pretty birds you can shoot."

Puffed with pride, Red Shell agreed. The man sang a song, and a birch hide canoe appeared, pulled by six swans. Red Shell marveled silently, but acted nonchalant. They stepped into the canoe, and the man guided the birds by song. They skimmed over the shining water and arrived at a large island.

Red Shell walked inland to the trees to hunt for birds. He noticed the gleam of bones in the tall grass, but because he was focusing upward he didn't examine them. After a time he heard singing, and returned to the shore. The man's canoe was already far from land. Red Shell yelled and waved, but the man didn't look back.

Night approached. Cold and hungry, Red Shell took shelter under the trees, and cried.

"Hiss," a faint voice said, "Be quiet."

Red Shell looked around. The skeleton of a man lying half-propped against a tree beckoned. "Poor boy," it said, "I fell for the same trick, but I can help if you will do me a service." It pointed to a tree. "Dig on the west side of that tree, and bring me the pouch containing smoking mixture, a pipe, and flint."

Petrified, Red Shell didn't move at first, but the skeleton assured him it would do him no harm. He followed its instructions, and lit the stone pipe. The skeleton inhaled and the smoke wafted out of its ribs. Mice squeaked and scurried from their nests in its bones. It sighed. "That's better." Its empty eye sockets turned to gaze at Red Shell. "Now, prepare! A giant will

come soon with dogs to hunt you. Jump in and out of water many times to disguise your scent, and then hide in a hollow tree at the far side of the island. When he leaves return to me."

Red Shell thanked the skeleton and ran to find the hollow tree trunk. Just as he discovered it, the earth shook and the barking of three vicious dogs rang out.

A voice boomed, "Find the boy!"

Red Shell took off like a shot arrow and ran a crooked path through the island, crossing the stream several times. The frustrated howls of the dogs were loud, but they didn't gain on him. Finally, he dashed for the hollow trunk, and hid for the night.

By the morning, the giant was furious and he blamed the dogs. With a single blow of his club he killed one of the animals, ripped off its skin, and ate it raw. After his grisly feast, the giant drove the two whimpering dogs into his canoe, and departed.

Once it was safe, Red Shell returned to the skeleton.

"You survived!" it said with a note of surprise. "Remain brave! Tonight the man who brought you here will return to drink your blood. Go to the shore, and dig a pit in the sand. Lie in it and cover yourself. When he gets out of his canoe, jump into it, and say "Come swans, let us go home." *Do not turn or look at him!* When you are free, think of me sometimes."

Red Shell did as the skeleton instructed. At dusk he heard singing. He waited in his dark pit for footsteps to pass by and peeked out.

The man shouted, "Boy, I heard you evaded the giant. Impressive! You are worthy of a great honor. Come out of hiding."

Red Shell leaped up and into the canoe. He called out "Come swans, let us go home," and the swans immediately pulled the canoe into the lake. Behind him the man shouted and entreated him to return, but despite great temptation, Red Shell refused to look at him.

The swans guided him to a small island, where the man had a comfortable, well-stocked home hidden in a cave. After his adventures, Red Shell was glad to eat and rest on the couch of bobcat skins.

The next morning Red Shell searched the man's belongings, and discovered a beautiful shell necklace he recognized as his sister's. He grabbed a knife, a bow and arrows, and ran to the canoe. He ordered the swans to take him to the island. He was determined to find out about Wild Sage.

When Red Shell arrived the first thing he noticed was a wide trail of gore. He followed it and discovered the bloody remains of the man who had tricked him to the island. The boy hurried to the skeleton to discover what happened.

After another smoke, the skeleton related the terrible fight between the giant and the man over the absence of Red Shell, and the loss of the magic canoe. "The giant set his dogs on him! Then he ate the man's heart. But I heard something else: the giant took your sister as his slave!"

Red Shell reeled in shock, for he had believed his sister dead. The skeleton directed him to travel east and stop at the island with three large rocks where the giant resided. "After that, return here and I hope you will perform a task for me."

Red Shell agreed gladly, and jumped into the canoe, excited at the prospect of finding his sister. By evening, he spotted the giant's island, and he hid the canoe under overhanging trees. Taking care, he scouted for a trail, and found one that led to a stream where Wild Sage was drawing water.

He ran up to her and she dropped her container in surprise. They hugged and cried at their unexpected and joyful reunion.

Then the earth shook and dogs howled, and the brother and sister froze. The giant roared when he saw them. "You won't escape this time! I'll have both of you in my pot tonight!"

Red Shell and Wild Sage ran like deer to the canoe, leaped in, and pushed off. The giant thundered after them. At the shore he seized a fishing line with a large hook, and flung it at the canoe.

It landed inside and he pulled the canoe back to shore. Quick as a flash, Red Shell cut the line with his knife, and laughed at the giant.

Enraged, the giant lay down and began to drink the lake water so fast that the canoe was drawn towards him. Red Shell picked up his bow and sighted carefully. He shot the arrow. It pierced the giant's eye and drove into his skull. The giant's mouth opened in shock, and his life, and the water, drained out of him.

Red Shell and Wild Sage arrived at the island of the skeletons at dawn. The skeleton congratulated them, and asked them to gather all of the bones on the island and lay them side-by-side in one place. It took several days because there were so many. When they were finished, the skeleton instructed them to say, "Dead folk, arise."

Red Shell and Wild Sage held hands, and said together: "Dead folk, arise!"

Miraculously, the bones clicked together into whole skeletons and human flesh knitted over them. Soon there was a group of men standing before them, happily surprised at their resurrection. The talkative skeleton was now a handsome man called White Eagle.

It took many trips by canoe to transport everyone from the island. Then Red Shell and Wild Sage ran to their uncle's longhouse.

When he saw them, the stoop left his shoulders and light returned to his life. His family, the last of his tribe, were together again.

With their new friends crowded into their longhouse, they celebrated all night and swapped stories of their adventures and trials.

The next morning some men returned home, but many elected to stay. They all helped erect more longhouses, and within weeks, a new village was born.

# Godmother Death

Many years ago, a farmer called Harold faced a dilemma: his wife Mary had just given birth to their thirteenth child, a boy named Cedric. Because Harold and Mary were so poor, and had so many children, they could not find anyone to agree to be a godparent to the baby. Also, many considered the number thirteen unlucky.

Harold swore not to return home until he had found a suitable candidate for his son. He left his house full of clamouring children and a wife not fit enough to leave her bed, and set out on his quest – by way of the local pub.

All Harold's neighbors knew his quandary, and while many of them felt obliged to buy him a congratulatory drink, few wanted to be responsible for supporting young Cedric. By midnight Harold was merry but still lacking a godparent. It was a fine night, so he took a ramble through the village, searching for people too polite to refuse the "honor."

As he weaved through the crossroads at the center of the village, he spotted a striking woman: tall, gaunt, and wearing a hooded cape. Harold imagined her eyes gleamed with intelligence and wit, but if he had been sober, he might have

thought there was a frightening directness to her gaze.

"My Lady," he called out, and she swiveled her face to look at him properly.

"You see me," she replied.

"As clear as that carriage!" he said, pointing to a well-appointed black carriage.

She laughed, and Harold fancied it sounded like the bark of a vixen. "Well, Mr. Sharp Sight, what can I do for you?"

Harold outlined his need, and the woman nodded. "I will take care of Cedric. But first I must tell you that I am Death."

In his intoxicated state, Harold was unable to grasp her meaning. Death put him in her carriage, which was drawn by four red-eyed horses and driven by a shadow in a top hat and high-collared coat.

After a fast, wild drive, the carriage veered off the road and into a tunnel. Death helped a bewildered Harold out of the vehicle and led him down a steep incline. At the bottom, he beheld a wondrous sight: an enormous cavern, lit entirely by millions of candles of all different sizes.

"Each candle represents the life of a person," Death

told Harold. His eyes were round with shock. "The tallest are those of newborn infants, like your Cedric. The shortest represent those I shall reap from their lives quite soon." The candle flames danced and flung up shadow scenes of people's lives.

Harold could not resist the question: "Where is my candle?"

Without comment she led him through rows of flickering flames and pointed to a glimmering stub, near to extinction.

Suddenly clear-headed, Harold cried out, "But ... my wife, my children! I can't die now. Please, Mistress, light a new candle on this spot."

She pulled the hood away from her face, and Harold stepped back from her penetrating stare. "That is impossible," she said. "Each person has an allotted time on this earth. Sometimes even babies are born with only a thin disc of wax. You'll be glad to know that Cedric's candle will burn long. I will light it now."

As she turned her back on Harold he picked up the biggest candle he could find, lit it from the remnant that represented his life and put the tall burning candle in its place.

Death set alight the wick of Cedric's candle, and without turning said, "Harold, I will stand by your son and teach him a trade, but you will regret that action."

She seized his elbow in an ice-cold grip and escorted him to her carriage. When they arrived at Harold's home, she entered and all the children fell quiet and became well mannered. Death met Mary and inquired about her health, and the two spoke for some time.

The next day, Death held Cedric in her arms and accepted the responsibility of being his godmother while Harold watched them, nervous.

When Cedric turned eighteen, his godmother took part in his birthday celebration. He was the youngest, so it was a modest party, since his brothers and sisters had their own homes and were busy with careers. Mary lit a candle on a simple teacake and presented it to Cedric to blow out. Harold watched the scene with a touch of dread. It reminded him too much of Death's underground chamber. But Death smiled, and when Cedric blew out the candle they all clapped.

Death took Cedric to a forest and pointed to the herbs and plants growing there. She described their medicinal values, and informed him that from now on they would sing out their properties when he was searching for a cure.

She also explained, "If you notice me standing at the bottom of a patient's bed, there is hope for a cure as long as your skill is sufficient. If I stand by the head of the afflicted, however, I am there to claim a life, and no intervention will ward off my chilling hand."

Cedric followed his godmother's advice and became a renowned healer. He grew wealthy, and bought a great house. His parents moved in with him, although his mother sickened a short time later. One morning, Cedric was tending to his mother when Godmother Death appeared at the head of Mary's bed. Death nodded at him, and Cedric understood that he could do no more for his mother.

Harold noticed his son glance up and grow serious, and he guessed what it portended. He clung to Cedric and begged him to save Mary, but Cedric dared not deprive his godmother of her due. Mary passed into Death's realm that evening. Harold hardened his heart against Cedric, and as time passed they spoke less frequently and about nothing of consequence.

Harold grew frail and weak, but he did not die. Eventually he was confined to bed, where he lay, a thin and wasted man, and watched life continue outside his window.

Late one night Cedric received an urgent summons: the King's only daughter was seriously ill. The King had declared that anyone who cured her would earn her hand in marriage and, eventually, the throne.

Cedric left his father in the care of a trusted servant and rushed to the bedside of the ailing girl. When he saw her beauty and youth, his desire to cure her increased tenfold. The King paced up and down the room, desperate. Just as Cedric decided upon the correct medicine, he heard a rustling of skirts and his godmother emerged. She slowly walked to the head of bed of the stricken princess, and stopped. Death regarded her godson with a resolute and terrible expression.

Cedric didn't flinch.

He whispered first to the King, who shot him a strange look but nodded. Four soldiers were ordered into the room and positioned at each corner of the bed. Upon a signal from Cedric, they picked up the bed and rotated it so that Godmother Death was standing at the girl's feet. Cedric quickly administered a cure to the Princess, and immediately her eyes flickered open and she sat up.

The King and his retinue swarmed around the girl, delighted and eager to hear her speak. But when they turned

to congratulate Cedric, they couldn't find him.

In his moment of transgression, Godmother Death had promptly transported Cedric to her cave of candles.

"You were trained to alleviate pain and grant people a healthy lifespan," she scolded. "I alone decide who lives and dies. I will not be thwarted." She pointed to a tiny candle with a dying flame. "That was the King's daughter's candle. I must fulfill my duty."

Before Cedric could plead for the young woman's life, Godmother Death reached forward and snuffed out the light between her thumb and forefinger.

In that instant, Cedric fell down dead.

His corpse was found in the Princess's bedchamber and was returned to Harold, who was sadly too feeble to attend his youngest son's funeral. He wept and prayed for Godmother Death to ease him into her domain, but his candle continued to burn in her cavern.

By way of thanks, the King ordered that Harold receive the best of care. For many years Harold lay in bed, slowly declining, watching his children and grandchildren die before him. And as much as he yearned for death, every day he wished far more that he had forgiven his son.

One morning Godmother Death appeared at his bedside.

"Will you take me now?" he gasped.

As a reply she placed her frigid fingers on his eyelids and drew them down.

He heard the squeal of a newborn, and opened his eyes to blinding light.

# The Seven Ravens

There was once a couple who had seven sons, and as much as they loved their boys, they often wished for a daughter. One day, while driving cattle through a field, the husband found a copper ring in the middle of a circle of red-capped mushrooms and decided it must be lucky. Holding it in his palm, he made a wish for a daughter and then gave the ring to his wife, telling her it was charmed.

Soon after, his wife became pregnant and the entire household waited for the arrival of the new child with great excitement. To everyone's delight, a girl was born, but the labor had been long and difficult, and the baby girl —whom they named Una — was sickly and unwell. A house full of boys is rarely quiet, but during this time they all spoke in hushed tones and hung about the house, hoping Una would get better. All of them wanted to do something to help.

Finally, their father decided to set them a task to get them out from under his feet. He gathered all the boys, and instructed the oldest to take their pewter pitcher and fill it with water from the stream that flowed through the field in which he had discovered the ring. He explained that the water had healing properties and could save his sister.

Upon hearing this, *all* the boys clamored to go, and created a loud fuss. Their father pretended to accede to their demands, and asked them to complete the task together. The boys raced to the river, eager to be the one who would save their sister. But they fell to arguing over who would draw water from the stream. Soon all of them were grabbing at the pitcher. A tugging match ensued, and in the struggle the pitcher tumbled into the river with a splash and disappeared.

The boys were silent for a time. Their parents didn't have much money and the pitcher was a favorite of their father's. They then squabbled amongst themselves over who was to blame, but really they were putting off returning home and reporting their failure to their father. They had nothing else in which to carry water home.

The day wore on into evening, and back home the boys' father became impatient. He was caring for his wife, who was still worn out from childbirth, and watching over his frail baby girl. He imagined that the boys were out playing instead of completing the simple chore he had given them.

He decided to place the ring under Una's pillow in the hope that it would effect a cure. While it was in his hand he looked out of the window and saw ravens swooping in the sky. He frowned, and gripped the ring hard. "I wish those foolish sons of mine were all turned into ravens!" he declared.

In that moment there was a rushing of wings, and seven black ravens flew past the window.

The boys never returned home. The husband and wife were distraught, but during the long months of futile searches their little girl was a comfort to them. Una recovered and thrived, but she grew up thinking that she was an only child, for her parents were careful never to mention her brothers.

From a young age, Una had a fiercely independent nature and tended to wander off to explore anything that took her fancy. Her parents were overly-protective, and attempted to watch her constantly and protect her from everything. For some children this might have inculcated a fearful attitude toward the world, but for Una it only made her more determined to discover what she was missing.

She learned when to be quiet and pay attention for opportunities to slip away, how to force a lock, and the best way to climb trees and ropes. Among the neighboring children she was known as the best person to count on if you wanted to get in or *out* of mischief.

One day, when Una was much older, she was in the middle of an argument with her best friend, when she blurted out, "Why should I listen to you? You drove your seven brothers away when you were born!"

Una questioned her parents. They admitted that her brothers had been missing since the day they went to fetch water to heal her. They assured her that it was not her fault, but Una could not rid herself of the notion that she was responsible for their disappearance. She decided she would search the world for them and would not rest until her family was reunited.

She knew the story of the magic ring, and also that her parents never dared hold it and use it. She made it her mission to find it. Whenever she was alone in the house, Una searched for it, and after several weeks discovered it beneath a loose flagstone in the floor. She tucked it into her pocket.

Una packed food and belongings, left her parents a note, and set out to find her brothers.

She traveled far and wide but could find no mention of her brothers anywhere. Finally, she consulted a seer, who told Una to go to the Sun, the Moon, or the stars, for they watched perpetually and surely one of them would know what had happened to her brothers.

Una journeyed to the west, through a scorched desert, to the domain of the Sun. When she arrived at his kingdom, the Sun radiated such fury and heat that Una was forced to run away before he destroyed her.

Una traveled east to the realm of the Moon. She walked through a barren, freezing landscape in darkness. But at the Temple of the Moon, Una discovered that the icy monarch was haughty and contemptuous, and refused to divulge any information about Una's brothers. The girl used all her tricks

> She traveled far and wide but could find no mention of her brothers anywhere.

to escape the Moon's influence, and set her sights north, to the land of the stars.

Una took passage on a ship and journeyed across the sea. After weeks of high waves and the taste of brine, she arrived upon the shore of the stars.

Each star sat on a throne in their firmament, and their glimmering lights were mesmerizing. They welcomed Una, and she rested among them, listening to their stories, for they loved to tell tales. Finally, the glorious Morning Star arrived and sat upon her throne. She told Una that her brothers had been enchanted and changed into ravens, but each evening they returned to a glass mountain and transformed into humans to share a meal together. At dawn, they became

ravens again. "If you discover their home, and partake of their food and drink before they sup, you will break the spell."

The Morning Star also gave Una a chicken leg, for the door to the mountain would not open without a key of flesh.

Reluctantly, Una took her leave of the stars and voyaged back across the sea. For many more years she searched for the glass mountain, for it moved location regularly. At last, to the south, she heard of a new sighting and made her way to it.

She found the sparkling mountain late one afternoon, and stood before it, shading her eyes, thrilled to be so near the end of her quest. She reached into her bag, and to her horror realized that during her adventures she had lost the chicken leg. Una had no key with which to open the door.

She could not risk waiting, in case the mountain moved again. Mustering up her courage, Una drew her knife and cut off the little finger on her left hand. Crying, she bound the bleeding stump with a string and inserted her severed finger into the lock.

The door opened.

She walked through a tunnel and came to a warren of rooms. Opening one door, she discovered a kitchen, and inside was a little man making a meal. He didn't seem disturbed by her sudden appearance, but asked what she wanted.

"I am looking for my seven brothers, who take the form of ravens by day," she told him.

"The Lord Ravens aren't home presently," he replied, "but you may wait for them in their dining hall. I am just making their meal."

Una followed the man into a room, where a table was set with seven plates and cups. After he had laid out the food, he left. Una sampled every plate and drank from each cup as quickly as possible. As she was finishing, Una heard the rushing of wings, followed by the voices of men.

She dropped the copper ring in the final cup and hid in a cupboard to watch. The seven brothers strolled into the room, chatting among themselves, and sat at the table.

Instantly they noticed that their meals had been sampled, and wondered aloud if some new trick had befallen them. But the youngest brother saw the ring in his cup and held it up for all of them to see.

"It is the magic ring," they declared. "Has our sister broken the spell at last?"

At that, Una burst out of the cupboard and into the joyful arms of her brothers. For a long time they exchanged stories of the adventures they had experienced. Best of all, when the sun rose they remained in human form.

Their exile was over.

Una and her brothers set out for home, singing with glad voices.

# The Tiger Chest

In the ancient city of Rahmatabad, there lived a wealthy rajah who was preoccupied by the fact that he never had a son. His only child, Princess Rashmi, was the jewel of his heart. She was not only beautiful, but a talented sitar player, and it was said she could charm the birds and beasts with her singing and playing. In fact, she loved animals, and was always adopting orphaned or injured creatures – her rooms in the palace were referred to as Rashmi's menagerie.

Above all her pets, Rashmi loved her pet monkey Vira the most. He was a black-faced grey-furred monkey that was so clever many people suggested he must be a disciple of the great monkey god Hanuman. He was always by Rashmi's side, and seemed to understand her every word.

When Rashmi was a child, she was betrothed to the son of the Rajah of Dilaram, now a young man called Prince Narendra. As was common they never met, although pictures of each other had been exchanged. As time went on Rashmi became more curious about her fiancé, and one day she sent Vira to Narendra's palace with a message for him. Over the following years the monkey often ran between the two palaces, swapping notes and small trinkets between the couple.

As Rashmi grew up, her father realized that inevitably she would marry and leave him, and it caused him much anguish. He became more devout, fasting and praying, and observing all the feast days in the hope that he and his wife would have another child. One day, rumors of a holy man of unprecedented wisdom reached his ears and the rajah set out to meet him.

The Yogi Amrit sat every day under a tree on the outskirts of Rahmatabad, and seemed indifferent to the blazing son or the drenching rain. He ate sparingly and spoke infrequently. Mostly, he sat in his saffron-colored robes, staring straight ahead, and clicked his prayer beads through his fingers.

When the rajah visited, the yogi gave him his full attention, and assured the rajah that with the right devotions, another child was possible. The rajah traveled to consult the yogi with increasing regularity. Several weeks later, the yogi mentioned he was considering moving to another town. On the spot the rajah offered to build the yogi a permanent shrine, with extra rooms for him and his pupils, and a walled courtyard. After many protests Yogi Amrit gave in, and the rajah built him a wonderful home next to his palace.

Rashmi had heard much about the yogi, and badgered her father to meet him. The rajah refused, explaining the yogi was too busy. Rashmi noticed her father was spending less time with her, and did everything the yogi advised. She decided she should see the great man herself.

Rashmi was never allowed outside the palace grounds without guards, so she disguised herself as one of her handmaidens, and veiled her face. To distract the guards, she instructed Vira to pelt the guards with nuts from one of the trees overhanging the palace walls. She was able to walk through the gates without being recognized while the guards cursed at Vira, as he hopped up and down in the tree.

Rashmi sat outside the yogi's new house with other devotees until his pupils emerged to select those who would be allowed in for a special consultation. She noticed that the best-dressed people or pretty girls got preference. She lowered her veil a little and one of the pupils tapped her on her arm to indicate she was one of the lucky ones.

After a time, she was brought in for her private consultation. The yogi offered her water, and since the day had been exceptionally hot, Rashmi accepted a cup from him. But when she dropped her veil to drink she noticed his expression changed.

"You are an extremely attractive woman," he said, and moved to sit beside her. "I feel the urge to bless you." He reached out and took her hand.

Unused to anyone laying a hand upon her, Rashmi pulled out of his grip and leaped up. "I did not give you permission to touch me," she said.

He fixed her with a terrible glare, and Rashmi understood instantly that this was a dangerous man who was unused to being thwarted.

"You silly fool," he said, "Do as I say or there will be terrible consequences."

Rashmi's eyes flashed in fury. "I am the Princess Rashmi, and *you* will pay me respect."

The yogi laughed, and grabbed the princess, pulling her close. "A word from me can bring even the mighty low." He attempted to kiss her.

Rashmi slapped him, and ran for the door to the walled courtyard. The yogi pursued her, but Rashmi was young and quick and was climbing over the wall by the time he reached the garden. He picked up one of his pupil's spears and threw it at the princess. It sliced across her calf, leaving a long wound. Rashmi stifled her cry and threw herself over the wall. She hit the ground hard, and limped home to the palace, keeping careful watch for signs of the yogi or his students.

At home, Rashmi washed and bound up her wound and pondered what she should do—but the yogi was already hatching a plot. That evening, the rajah came to visit the yogi, but he refused to speak. He clicked his prayer beads and said nothing until the rajah worked himself up into a lather of concern.

"I have bad news," the yogi said, finally. "There is a creature living among us who can bring destruction upon all of Rahmatabad."

The rajah staggered back in surprise. "What is this thing, and how can we destroy it?"

The yogi wore a solemn expression. "It takes the form of a beautiful woman, but it is really an evil spirit. Because of my training I saw through its illusion. It has eyes like coals of fire, a mouth full of fangs, and talons on its fingers. It would have consumed me except my powers were too great. I wounded it before it left."

The rajah's eyes widened in horror throughout the yogi's tale, for he was a superstitious man. "How will mere men recognize it? Advise me and I will do all that you ask."

"She will be a beautiful virgin, but with a spear wound on her leg. Once you discover her, imprison her.

I know how to deal with her."

Greatly disturbed by the idea of a demon living among them, the rajah alerted his soldiers to conduct a search of all the young women in the city. After two days, the demon had not been found. At that point, one of the yogi's pupils reminded the captain that the royal apartments had not been checked.

The princess's wound was discovered, much to her father's shock. Rashmi was confined to her rooms, but the rajah was certain it was a mistake, and he hurried to notify the yogi.

The yogi let the rajah speak for a little, and with utter confidence and a calm demeanor, he informed the rajah that his daughter had been stolen from him when she was a child and replaced with an evil spirit. He pointed out her unusual powers of voice and her ability to control animals. Finally, he suggested it was her demonic presence that prevented the rajah from having any more children.

The yogi was so persuasive, and his argument so compelling, that after a time the rajah came to believe him. He agreed to allow the yogi to deal with Rashmi as he saw fit.

The yogi ordered two carpenters to come to his chamber secretly, and explained how they should construct a chest that was so well made it would not let in any air or water.

Rashmi had been sending Vira to spy on what was

happening. She could not understand all the monkey's miming and screeches, but she knew that danger was fast approaching. She wrote a note for Prince Narendra, and instructed Vira to watch what happened to her, and after that deliver the note to her fiancé.

The soldiers burst into her room, and dragged her from the palace. Her father stayed in his room praying, and tried to pretend he could not hear the cries of his beloved daughter.

Rashmi was shoved inside the chest and special pegs were used to seal it shut. The chest was cast into the river, and it bobbed downstream. Once he witnessed what happened to his mistress, Vira scampered across rooftops and swung through trees until he found Prince Narendra. Upon reading the note the prince saddled his horse and galloped with his solders after the leaping monkey.

They spotted the chest quickly with Vira's help. Narendra dove into the water without hesitation and his soldiers followed. They hauled out the crate and opened it. Rashmi had almost suffocated and was terrified after being locked up in such a small space, but there was compensation in seeing Narendra for the first time.

He put her on his horse, and carried her to his palace, where his family treated her as a daughter. The next morning over breakfast, they discussed what to do. Vira had a place of honor by Rashmi's side.

"I heard you captured a tiger recently," Rashmi said to Narendra's father. "Seal it up in the chest, and throw it into the river. I believe the yogi has not finished with me."

They did as she suggested, and indeed, the yogi had told two of his students he'd had a prophetic dream, and to watch the river for a magic chest floating downriver.

When the pupils spotted it turning in the water, they once again marveled at their guru's prescience. They heaved it out of the river, put it on a cart, and brought it back to the yogi.

When he received delivery of it, the yogi ordered his pupils to leave the room, and not enter no matter what noise they heard.

The yogi smiled, and picked up a silken cord, planning to strangle the princess. He opened the lid.

The furious tiger exploded out of the chest. Its huge paws swatted the yogi and opened large gashes in his chest. The smell of blood further enraged the beast and it ripped out the yogi's throat with one vicious snap of its massive jaws.

Outside, the yogi's pupils trembled at the growls and screams coming from their master's room. They imagined him subduing a demon, and waited for hours before they dared open the door. As they entered the room, the tiger bounded past them and raced for the safety of the forest. Petrified by the sudden appearance of the beast, the students carefully peeked in the door.

> He suggested it was her demonic presence that prevented the rajah from having any more children.